U0094057

哈福

哈福

Good English in 5 min.

5分鐘
征服英文法

附
MP3

張瑪麗◎著
Doris Shetely◎校訂

哈福

5 分鐘征服英文法 ⋯⋯⋯⋯⋯⋯⋯

　　你是否還記得，上國中時開始學英語時的興奮和想學好英語的豪情，這麼多年了，你是否達成當年的願望，能說得一口好英語，可以輕鬆自如地從國外的報章雜誌或是書籍吸收最新的知識，而在工作場合嶄露頭角，還是已經望英語而生畏，但是，仍然對英語餘情未了，真想能夠把英語征服，如果你還有雄心，那就讓我來幫你一圓當初的心願吧。

英語贏在每天 5 分鐘

　　要學好英語不能把英語當作一門學問來研究，想想你是怎麼學中文的，我想大家學中文都是一樣的，那就是每天聽、每天看、每天說，學英語也應該是這樣學的，記得，英語是一種語言，你是要用英語來跟別人溝通的，所以每天都該說幾句，聽幾句，累積到一定的程度，英語就好像你說話的另一種語言，可以隨時輕鬆開口說的。要重新拼英語，不需要從很高深的 Time 或是 CNN 新聞節目開始，我們先複習一下你以前學過卻已經忘記的，所謂溫故而知新，把基礎打好了，開口說流利的英語也就輕鬆可得。

　　為了幫助想學英語的朋友，美國 AA Bridgers 公司特別製作了這一套「5 分鐘英語學習書」，我們從最基礎文法教起，每一單元的重點我們還是會提到文法名詞，文法名詞是讓你溫故用

的，學習的重點是在如何說流利的英語，所以每個例句都是講英語一定會用到的句子，為了溫習，也為了測試自己還有多少實力，你可以先看中文翻譯，試試看會不會該句英語。

　　你只要每天花個五分鐘的時間，看看我對每個動詞的說明，把每個例句都好好的思考一番，瞭解最基本的動詞的用法，平常說英語應該都沒有問題了。

要注意　　我一再強調的，英語是一種語言，是用來說的，要學會說英語，先要聽聽看美國人怎麼說，我們就跟著怎麼說，你說出口的英語自然道地流利，我們每本書都有美國老師錄製的學習光碟，每天聽一聽，嘴巴跟著唸，唸順了英語就是你的另一種語言了。

基本文法是學好英語的磐石

　　你是否常覺得學習那麼多年的英語，下了那麼多的功夫，英語還是跟你無緣，你跟英語之間就好像有一道很深的鴻溝，怎麼也跨不過去，你知道嗎？其實你在讀了「5分鐘英語學習書」，瞭解英語的基本句型，然後再把最基本的動詞學會，你的英語自然會突飛猛進。

1

answer
['ænsɚ]

有人問你問題，你可以 answer 他的問題，你也可以拒絕 answer；至於有人打電話來，就好像有人用電話在叫你一樣，你去接電話就是去 answer the phone；有人在敲門或是按門鈴，你是否一面往門邊走去，一邊喊著，來了來了，你是在回答那個人的敲門，所以，你去應門，也就是去 answer the door；有人寫信給你，你就會 answer 他的 letter。

動詞三態 answer, answered, answered

精選例句

回答

* Did he answer your question?
（他有沒有回答你的問題？）

* You still haven't answered my question.
（你還是沒有回答我的問題。）

* He answered me with a smile.
（他回給我一個微笑。）

	the phone. （接電話。）
answer	the door. （應門。）
	someone's letter. （回信。）

接電話

* Shall I answer the phone?
（你要我接電話嗎？）

應門

* Don't answer the door while your parents are not home.
（你的父母不在的時候，不要應門。）

* Will you answer the door?
（你去應門好嗎？）

* Can someone answer the door, please?
（誰有空去應門好嗎？）

回信

* Have you answered Mary's letter yet?
（你給瑪莉回信了嗎？）

2

ask
[æsk]

你跟對方提出問題，問她哪兒去啦，問他為什麼遲到，不管你跟對方提什麼問題問，都是 ask 他一個問題；至於請求幫忙，也是 ask 對方願意不願意幫忙；提出邀約，也是 ask 對方願意不願意接受你的邀請；還有，對方要跟你買某樣東西，你提出價錢，也是 ask 對方付這個價錢那才要賣。

動詞三態 ask, asked, asked

精選例句

問問題

* "Where are you going?" she asked.
（她問，「你要去哪裡？」）

* Can I ask you a question?
（我可以問你一個問題嗎？）

* She asked the students their names.
（她問學生的名字。）

* Go and ask John if she can come.
（去問約翰她能不能去。）

請求幫忙

* If you need help, you have to ask.
（如果你需要幫忙，你就得提出要求。）

* Ask John to give you a ride.
（去要求約翰載你。）

* Ask your brother if we could use his computer.
（去問你哥哥，我們可不可以用他的電腦。）

要價

* How much did she ask for the diamond ring?
（這顆鑽戒她要賣多少錢？）

邀請

* Do you think it's okay for me to ask her out?
（你想我邀她出去好嗎？）

* He asked her out to dinner, but she had other plans.
（他邀她去吃晚餐，但是她有其他的事。）

3

begin
[bɪˈgɪn]

不管是小孩開始走路，開始說話，或是天開始下雨，你開始在某個公司上班，學校開始上課，宴會從幾點開始，只要有事情開始了，這個開始的英語就是 begin

動詞三態 begin, began, begun

精選例句

開始

* Yesterday the baby began to walk.
（昨天，嬰兒開始走路。）

* Let's begin at page 10.
（我們從第十頁開始。）

* At last the guests began to arrive.
（客人終於開始來了。）

* We began to wonder if the bus would ever arrive.
（我們開始懷疑公車是否會來。）

* I began working in my present job two years ago.
（我兩年前開始在目前這個工作上班。）

* The party begins at 7:30.
（宴會七點半開始。）

* My cold began with a sore throat.
（我的感冒從喉嚨痛開始。）

 **這句話英語怎麼說**

☛ 有人在敲門，你跟你先生說，你去應門好嗎，這句話英語怎麼說？

☛ 有人在敲門，你正在廚房裡忙著，你就提高聲量，大聲叫道，誰有空去應門好嗎？這句話英語怎麼說？

☛ 你有問題要問約翰，你要跟他說，我可以問你一個問題嗎？這句話英語怎麼說？

☛ 你知道約翰喜歡瑪麗，你就問約翰，你有沒有約她出去，這句話英語怎麼說？

☛ 今晚瑪麗家有個宴會，朋友問你宴會幾點開始，你說宴會七點半開始，這句話英語怎麼說？

☛ 大家要一起討論功課，你說，我們從第五頁開始吧，這句話英語怎麼說？

這句話英語怎麼說

＊ 你去應門好嗎？	Will you answer the door?
＊ 誰有空去應門好嗎？	Can someone answer the door?
＊ 我可以問你一個問題嗎？	Can I ask you a question?
＊ 你有沒有約她？	Did you ask her out?
＊ 宴會從七點半開始。	The party begins at 7:30.
＊ 我們從第五頁開始。	Let's begin at page 5.

13

4

break
[brɛk]

break 的過去式和過去分詞是 broke 和 broken。有人打破了窗戶，打破了花瓶，打破了碗，就是 broke 這些東西，因為這些東西已經打破了，所以要用過去式 broke。有些東西雖然沒有被打破，卻壞了，不能用，例如：洗衣機、照相機、手錶、車子等東西，如果壞了，就是那樣東西 broke，或 has broken。如果是約翰把東西弄壞呢，那就是 John broke 這樣東西或 John has broken 這樣東西。

男孩子到了十二、三歲聲音就開始變的低沈，我們說那個男孩子在變聲，英語就是說他的 voice broke。

break 是打破、打斷的意思，所以大家休息去吃午飯，就是把時間打斷，所以也是 break。

動詞三態 break, broke, broken

精選例句

打破；打斷

* Who broke the vase?
  （誰打破這個花瓶？）

* The thief broke a window and got into the house.
  （小偷打破窗戶，進去屋子裡。）

* Be careful not to break the glass.
  （小心不要打破玻璃。）

* She fell off the bicycle and broke her arm.
（她從腳踏車上摔下來，摔斷手臂。）

把東西弄壞

* Someone's broken my camera.
（有人把我的照相機弄壞了。）

* John broke all the toys he got.
（約翰把所有他得到的玩具都弄壞。）

* The TV broke. Could you have someone fix it?
（電視壞了，你能叫人來修理嗎？）

男孩子變聲

* I was in the school choir until my voice broke.
（我一直在學校合唱團，直到我變聲。）

毀壞

* The dam finally broke, and the waters flooded the town.
（水壩終於毀了，水淹沒這個城鎮。）

休息

* Let's break for lunch now.
（我們休息，吃午飯。）

break	ground（破土）
	a record（破紀錄）
	a promise（破誓言、食言）
	a code（破密碼）

- The mayor came to break ground for the new building.
  （市長來為新的大樓破土。）

- The movie broke all box-office records.
  （這部電影打破所有的票房紀錄。）

- He broke the world 100 meters record.
  （他打破世界一百米賽跑的紀錄。）

- Mary never breaks a promise
  （瑪麗從來沒有食言。）

break 輕鬆學

☑ John and Mary broke up.
　　約翰和瑪莉兩個人不再來往。

☑ Someone broke in and stole Mary's jewelry.
　　有人闖空門，偷走瑪莉的首飾。

☑ My watch has broken.
　　我的手錶壞了。

☑ John broke the vase.
　　約翰打破這個花瓶。

☑ Can you break a twenty-dollar bill?
　　我這一張 20 元紙幣，你能不能換成小鈔給我？

☑ She broke his heart.
　　她傷了他的心。

⚠ 每天五分鐘

⏱ 男女朋友不再繼續交往，兩人「吹了」的英語就是 break up。

⏱ break in 就是「進去某人家或某個地方偷東西」。

⏱ break 這個字可以當「東西壞了」的意思。

⏱ 某人打破了花瓶，打破了盤子的「打破」的英語就是 break。

⏱ break a dollar bill 就是把一塊錢換成零錢。

⏱ 讓別人很傷心，就是 break 那個人的 heart。

5

bring
[brɪŋ]

你在餐廳吃飯，要服務生拿些紙巾給你，就要跟他說 bring me some napkins；你家小孩從外面進來，淋得一身濕淋淋的，趕緊跟他說，站著別動，我會 bring you a towel。

bring 還可以做「隨身帶著」的意思，你出門之前，看天色陰霾，恐怕會下雨，你說 I bring an umbrella with me. 表示「我帶著一把傘。」

動詞三態 bring, brought, brought

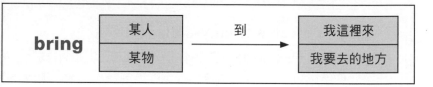

■ Would you bring me some napkins?
（請你拿一些紙巾給我？）

■ I left my book at your house. Could you bring it to school tomorrow?
（我的書留在你家。你明天可以帶去學校嗎？）

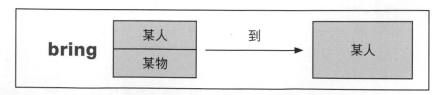

■ Hold on, I'll bring you a towel.
（別動，我拿條毛巾給你。）

■ They brought her everything she asked for.
（他們帶給她，她所要求的一切東西。）

↻ 隨身帶著書，帶著雨傘或某樣東西。
帶了某人去參加宴會，或帶了某人去某個地方。

◆ Did you bring any books to read?
（你有沒有帶書來讀？）

◆ I bring an umbrella with me in case it rains.
（我帶著一把傘，萬一下雨用得到。）

◆ John brought a friend to the party.
（約翰帶一個朋友去參加宴會。）

↻ 當有人邀你去參加宴會，你問對方需要你帶東西去嗎，以下是
一些很漂亮的說法，這種英語要多記多說，表示你很「上道」

◆ Is there anything I could bring?
（需要我帶什麼東西來嗎？）

◆ What shall I bring?
（我該帶什麼來？）

◆ Can I bring the drinks?
（我帶飲料來好嗎？）

Just bring yourself.
（你人來就好了。）

● 有人開宴會，邀請你去參加，或是有人邀請你到他家作客，我們總不好意思大剌剌的空手去，但是，帶什麼去好呢，你可以問問邀你去的主人 Is there anything I could bring?（需要我帶什麼東西來嗎？），或是問 What shall I bring?（我該帶什麼來？），有時主人會要求你帶飲料，或是水果啦，有時主人認為他什麼什麼都準備了，不需要你帶什麼東西去，他就會跟你說 Just bring yourself.（你人來就好。）

What brings you here?
（什麼風把你吹來了？）

● 如果有朋友忽然來訪，我們常會驚喜的問他，什麼風把你吹來了？這句話英語的說法就是 What brings you here?

 這句話英語怎麼說

☛ 你看到客廳的花瓶被打破了，不禁高聲問道，誰打破這個花瓶？這句話英語怎麼說？

☛ 你想看電視，卻發現電視機壞了，就說，電視機壞了，這句話英語怎麼說？

☛ 你家小孩洗完澡，濕淋淋的就從浴室走出來，你趕緊跟他說，別動，我拿條毛巾給你，這句話英語怎麼說？

☛ 瑪麗邀你到她家參加宴會，你不想空手而去，你就問瑪麗，我該帶什麼來？這句話英語怎麼說？

☛ 中午吃飯時間到了，你要大家休息，吃午飯，這句話英語怎麼說？

這句話英語怎麼說

* 誰打破這個花瓶？　　Who broke the vase?

* 電視機壞了。　　The TV broke.

* 我拿條毛巾給你。　　I'll bring you a towel.

* 請拿一些紙巾我好嗎？　　Would you bring me some napkins?

* 我該帶什麼來？　　What shall I bring?

* 我們休息，吃午飯。　　Let's break for lunch.

6

buy
[baɪ]

不管你要購買什麼東西，都是 buy，如果你已經買了，那就要用過去式 bought，至於有人告訴你一個消息，如果你相信了，那就是你 buy 他的消息，如果你不相信，那就是你 don't buy 他的消息。那麼你如果想請客，例如：請她吃飯或是請她喝飲料，是不是表示你要替她付飯錢或是飲料錢，也可以說你 buy 她這頓飯或是這杯飲料了。繼續引伸，有人做了壞事，要賄賂警察或是司法人員，那就要 buy 警察或是司法人員手上的權限，來幫你做事。

動詞三態 buy, bought, bought

buy			
購買	相信	賄賂	請客

精選例句

購買

* Where can I buy an antique desk?
（我在哪裡可以買到古董書桌？）

* I bought this watch for $20 at the sale.
（我在打折的時候用二十塊錢買到這個手錶。）

* If you're thinking of getting a new
computer, now is a good time to buy.
（如果你在考慮要買一部新電腦的話，現在是
買的好時機。）

* A dollar doesn't buy much these days.
（這年頭一塊錢買不到什麼東西。）

你跟男朋友約會，他竟然遲到了，而且，還給你一大堆理由，
什麼塞車啦，或是車子壞了一時沒辦法發動啦，如果你相信他
的理由，不跟他計較，那就算了，如果你不相信，就跟他說
I don't buy it.（別找理由了，我才不信呢。）

◆ Don't give me that excuse.
I don't buy it.
（別跟我說那個理由，我不相信。）

你買東西，就是付錢給對方，然後把東西拿回來，如果你付錢
給人，卻不是要買他的東西，而是要買他手上的權限，同樣也
是 buy，這樣的 buy，中文就叫做「賄賂」或「買通」。

◆ They say the judge was bought.
（聽說法官已經被收買了。）

🔄 buy 這個字就是付錢把東西拿回來的意思，如果，你想請女朋友喝杯飲料，也就是你想付錢替她買飲料，趕緊跟她說 Let me buy you a drink.

◆ Let me buy you a drink.
　（我請你喝一杯。）

🔄 你的老闆突然跟你要一份報告，但是你還沒做完，你又不願意跟老闆說你還沒做好，你只好趕緊找一些理由來 buy some time，然後趕快趕完好送給老闆。

🔄 你老爸要你把車子開去洗車，但是你竟然開了車子跟朋友去玩，結果你老爸打電話給你要用車子了，你只好跟他說，你迷路了，buy some time 以便趕快把車子洗好了，開回去給你老爸。

◆ Tell them we've got lost, it might buy us some time.
　（跟他們說我們迷路了，這樣我們可能爭取一點時間。）

buy 輕鬆學

☐ Where did you buy that watch?
　　你那支手錶在哪裡買的？

☐ I bought the desk for $100.
　　我以一百元買了這張桌子。

☐ She bought me a new car.
　　她買了一部新車給我。

☐ I sold it too cheap. I want to buy it back.
　　那樣東西我賣的太便宜，我想買回來。

☐ Can I buy you a drink?
　　我請你喝杯飲料好嗎？

☐ John tried to buy off the cops.
　　約翰想要買通警員。

每天五分鐘

🕐 大家都學過 buy 就是「購買某樣東西」的意思，這個字的過去式是 bought，你買了某樣東西，別人問你在哪裡買的，你的女朋友買了一部車子給你，你用一百塊錢買了一支手錶，當你說這些話時，東西都已經買了，英語說到這樣的句子，都得用過去式。

🕐 你想追女孩子，一開始，當然是先請她吃個飯，或是喝個飲料，請人吃飯或是喝飲料，也就是你出錢幫她買食物或是飲料，英語就是 buy 這個字。

🕐 買東西是 buy，你做了壞事，想買通警察或是法官，英語也是 buy。

7

call
[kɔl]

每個人都叫雜貨店的老闆「老張」，也就是說每個人都 calls him 老張，至於給新生兒取名字 John，或給家裡的小狗取名字 Cute，就是 call the baby John，或是 call the puppy Cute。call 除了是叫名字，取名字之外；一個人在大聲叫，也是 call，叫計程車就是 call a cab，打電話也是 call，如果你家來了壞人，或是出什麼事，你要叫警察，通常都是用打電話的，所以就說 call the police，不過你如果在大街上被搶，正好附近有警察在，你並不是打電話給警察，而是大聲 call（叫）警察了。

動詞三態 call, called, called

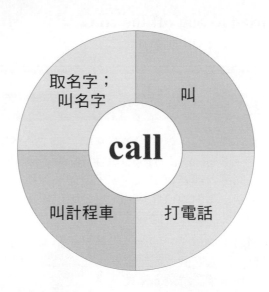

精選例句

| 取名字；叫名字 | * What do you want to call the new puppy?
（這隻小狗你要取什麼名字？） |

* His name is Bob but everyone calls him "Old daddy".
（他的名字是鮑勃，但是每個人都叫他「老爹」。）

叫

* I heard somebody calling.
（我聽到有人在叫。）

* Did somebody call my name?
（是不是有人叫我的名字？）

叫計程車

* We'll have to call a cab if the rain doesn't stop soon.
（如果雨不很快停的話，我們必須叫部計程車。）

打電話

* I'll call you later.
（我稍後再打電話給你。）

* I think we should call the doctor.
（我認為我們應該打電話給醫生。）

* She will call us from the airport when she arrives.
（她到的時候會從機場打電話給我們。）

* If you don't leave, I'll call the police.
（如果你不離開的話，我要叫警察。）

call 輕鬆學

☑ We called on Mary last week.
　　　　我們上星期去拜訪瑪莉。

☑ I'll call you back.
　　　　我會再打電話給你。

☑ He called me names again.
　　　　他又在罵我。

☑ John called in sick this morning.
　　　　約翰今天早上打電話來請病假。

☑ My English teacher calls the roll every day.
　　　　我的英文老師每天都點名。

☑ The game was called off because of the rain.
　　　　因為下雨的關係，比賽取消了。

❗ 每天五分鐘

⏱ call on 是「拜訪某人」的意思。

⏱ call back 是「給某人回電話」的意思。

⏱ call 某人 names，就是用難聽的話罵那個人，例如：罵他笨蛋、白痴或是其他不好聽的話。

⏱ call in sick 就是「打電話去請病假」的意思。

⏱ call the roll 就是「點名」的意思。

⏱ call off 就是「取消」的意思。

大家來說英語

call it a day

● 工作了一整天,該下班了,如果你是主管或是老闆,你想跟大家說,我看今天就做到這裡好了,大家可以下班了,你就可以跟大家說 Let's call it a day. 或是 Time to call it a day.

● 如果是你自己決定要下班回家了,其他的同事有人已經下班,有人還有工作還在繼續做,你只是想跟大家說你要走了,你就可以說,I'm going to call it a day.

call it a night

● 夜深了,一家人或許有人在看電視,有人在忙著做家事,有人還在看書,你認為大家該去睡覺了,你就可以招呼大家一聲說 Time to call it a night.,如果只是你自己想去睡覺了,你就可以跟大家說 I'm going to call it a night.

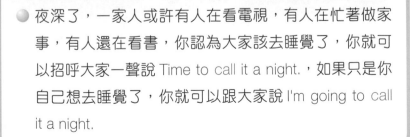

8

care
[kɛr]

你對你的事業、家庭在乎嗎，你對你的學業、比賽的成敗在乎嗎，如果你在乎，就是你 care，如果你不在乎，就是你 don't care。你如果在宴會上看到一個漂亮的女孩子，想邀她跳支舞，你該當問她說 Would you care for a dance? 這裡的 care 是「喜歡、想要」的意思，而你問她喜不喜歡的是 for a dance，如果你問她喜不喜歡 go to the movies（去看電影），要說 Would you care to go to the movies?

動詞三態 care, cared, cared

在乎；關心

care

想要

精選例句

在乎；關心

* She doesn't care what people think of her.
（她不在乎人們對她的看法。）

* I don't care whether we win or not.
（我不在乎我們會不會贏。）

* He cares about the quality of his work.
（他在乎他工作的品質。）

* I really care about her.
（我真的很關心她。）

* She cares nothing about your money.
（她並不在乎你的錢。）

想要

* Would you care to go to the movies with me?
（你要不要跟我去看電影？）

* I really don't care to see that movie.
（我真的不想去看那部電影。）

Would you care for a dance?
（要不要跳一支舞？）

● 你如果去參加舞會，看到了一個漂亮的小姐，你真想邀她與你共舞，你就可以走過去彬彬有禮的一鞠躬，一邊伸出你的右手做相邀狀，一邊說 Would you care for a dance?，小姐如果懂得英語，就知道你是在相邀共舞一曲了。

● care for 是「喜歡、想要」的意思，除了可以用在邀女孩子跳舞之外，也可以用在想拿個飲料給對方時，問她，Would you care for a drink?（你要喝什麼飲料嗎？）

I don't care.
（我才不在乎呢。）

● 美國小孩如果要脫口說出這句話時，通常會再考慮一下，可不可以說這句話，因為說了這句話，遇到嚴格的家長或是老師，說這句話的小朋友可能會挨罵，不管大人或小孩說這句話時，總有天不怕地不怕的氣概，例如：媽媽叫小孩小聲點，爺爺在睡覺，小孩可能回媽媽一句 I don't care. 這句話的意思就是說，我就是要大聲玩鬧，我才不管爺爺在睡覺呢，這時就看媽媽的態度了，是要任小霸王無法無天呢，還是要好好的教訓一番。

這句話英語怎麼說

- 你的男朋友約會遲到，到了之後，他說，他的車子壞了，沒辦法發動，你叫他別騙你了，你說，我不相信，這句話英語怎麼說？

- 你想約女同事去冰果室喝飲料，以便進一步跟她聊聊天，這句話英語怎麼說？

- 你在跟約翰講電話時，有另一通電話進來，是國際長途電話，你得先接聽這一通電話，你就跟約翰說，我稍後再打電話給你，這句話英語怎麼說？

- 大家在客廳裡看電視看到很晚，你要大家去睡覺了，這句話英語怎麼說？

- 在宴會上，你看到一個漂亮的女孩，你想邀她共舞一曲，這句話英語怎麼說？

- 有人邀你去看一部新上映的電影，你不喜歡那部電影，你要跟他說，我真的不想看那部電影。這句話英語怎麼說？

這句話英語怎麼說

* 我不相信。　　　　　　I don't buy it.

* 我請你喝杯飲料。　　　Let me buy you a drink.

* 我稍後再打電話給你。　I'll call you later.

* 我們去睡覺吧。　　　　Let's call it a night.

* 請跟我共舞一曲好嗎？　Would you care for a dance?

* 我真的不想看那部電影。

　　　　　　　　　　　I really don't care to see that movie.

9

carry
[ˈkærɪ]

carry 就是「帶著某樣東西或某人」的意思，帶著手提箱，身上帶著錢，手上抱著嬰孩，都是 carry。加以引伸，報紙上刊登某個消息，就是報紙上 carry 這個消息；電視台轉播球賽，就是電視台 carry 這場球賽；而你有保什麼保險就是你 carry 某樣保險，同樣的，一部車子如果有四年的保證，就是這部車子 carries 四年的保證，車子是第三人稱單數，carry 要改成 carries。

動詞三態　carry, carried, carried

carry
- 拿；抱
- 帶在身上
- 運送
- 刊登
- 電視轉播
- 有保險
- 有保證

拿；抱

精選例句

* Will you carry my bag, please?
（可以請你幫我拿袋子嗎？）

* She carried her baby in her arms.
（她抱著她的嬰孩在手上。）

帶在身上

* She always carries her purse.
（她總是帶著她的皮包。）

* Do you carry a pen?
（你有沒有帶筆？）

運送

* The large pipe carries water.
（這條大的管子是輸送水用的。）

刊登

* All the newspapers carried the news
of their divorce.
（所有的報紙都刊登他們離婚的消息。）

電視轉播

* He watched the football game,
carried live on ABC.
（他看由美國廣播公司實況轉播的足球賽。）

有保險

* Do you carry any life insurance?
（你有保人壽保險嗎？）

有保證

* That car carries a four-year warranty.
（那部車子有四年的保證。）

carry	攜帶病原	容納（物件、酒量）
	支撐	商店有賣某樣東西

攜帶病原

* Many serious diseases are carried by mosquitoes.

（很多嚴重的疾病是蚊子傳染的。）

容納（物件、酒量）

* The suitcase can carry enough clothes for two weeks.

（這個皮箱裝的下兩個星期需要的衣服。）

支撐

* How much weight will this bridge carry?

（這座橋的載重量是多少？）

商店有賣某樣東西

* Does your store carry black skirts?

（你們店裡有賣黑色的裙子嗎？）

carry 輕鬆學

☐ I never carry much money on me.
　　我身上從不帶很多錢。

☐ He was carrying a suitcase.
　　他帶著一個手提箱。

☐ He carries the backpack everywhere.
　　他到哪裡都背著背包。

☐ Although she carries her age well, she must be over fifty.
　　雖然她不顯老，但是她應該已超過五十歲。

☐ John can't carry the ball. He isn't organized enough.
　　不可以讓約翰負責。他不夠有條理。

☐ Do you think you can carry out the job?
　　你認為你能完成這個工作嗎？

每天五分鐘

🕐 carry one's age well 就是「不顯老」的意思。

🕐 carry the ball 就是「負責」的意思。

🕐 carry out 是「完成任務」或「完成指定作業」的意思。

10

catch
[kætʃ]

catch 就是「抓住」的意思，警察抓到小偷，你抓到一隻兔子，就是 catch 那個小偷，那隻兔子；若是考試作弊被老師抓到，雖然不像抓小偷或是抓兔子那樣實際上抓著，英文是 catch 這個字，中文也是說「抓到」；而你要趕火車、趕飛機、趕公車，好不容易趕上了，也可以說是 catch 到了，才可以上去；要是感冒了，也可以說「你是 catch（抓到）」感冒吧，否則感冒為什麼會上你身呢？

動詞三態 catch, caught, caught

抓到

catch

考試作弊，
被老師抓到

精選例句

抓到

* The police didn't catch the thief.
（警察沒有抓到小偷。）

* They caught a rabbit.
（他們抓到一隻兔子。）

| 考試作弊，被老師抓到 | * The teacher caught John cheating at the exam.
（老師抓到約翰考試作弊。） |

catch			
趕火車	趕公車	趕飛機	追趕人

■ We will have to hurry to catch the train.
（我們要快一點才能趕上火車。）

■ I have to catch the 3:00 flight to New York.
（我要去趕三點的飛機到紐約。）

■ John started to run, and Mary could not catch him.
（約翰開始跑，瑪莉趕不上他。）

catch a cold	感冒

■ You'd better put on a coat, or you'll catch a cold.
（你最好穿上大衣，否則你會感冒。）

■ I catch a cold every winter.
（我每年冬天都感冒。）

catch up	趕上

■ If you miss a lot of lessons, it's very difficult to catch up.
（如果你有很多課沒上，很難趕得上。）

11

come
[kʌm]

come 跟 go 這兩個字都是從某個地方到另一個地方，但是這兩個字走的方向是相反的，come 是從遠處來到「說話者」所在的地方，所以也有「到達」的意思。come 還可以是說從某個地方到「你說話的對象」所在的地方，例如：你問瑪麗，我可以到你家來看你嗎？你是要到瑪麗（瑪麗是你說話的對象）家，英語的說法是 Can I come and see you?

動詞三態 come, came, come

從	某個地方	**come**（來到）	說話者的地方
			你說話對象所在的地方

精選例句

來

* Come here.
　（過來。）

* Would you like to come to our party?
　（你要不要來參加我們的宴會？）

* Mary is coming later on.
　（瑪莉等一下會來。）

* Are you coming back Friday?
　（你星期五要回來嗎？）

* What day are your friends coming to dinner?
（你的朋友哪一天要來吃晚餐？）

* Why don't you come over Friday?
（你何不星期五過來我家？）

* Someone is coming to fix the TV.
（有人會來修理電視。）

* Did you come by plane or by train?
（你搭飛機還是乘火車來？）

抵達；
到達

* When does the train come?
（火車什麼時候到？）

去聽話者
的地方

* Can Mary come too?
（瑪莉也可以來嗎？）

* Can I come and see you tomorrow?
（我明天可以來看你嗎？）

come		
來的次序	排重要性名次	來自

來的次序

* Eight comes before nine.
（八在九的前面。）

* Nine comes after eight.
（九在八的後面。）

41

排重要性
名次

＊ My family always comes before anything.
（我的家庭是最重要的。）

＊ For John, his career always comes first.
（對約翰來說，事業最重要。）

＊ At the tournament, we came last.
（我們比賽得到最後一名。）

來自

＊ Mary comes from a large family.
（瑪莉來自一個大家庭。）

＊ Where do you come from?
（你從哪裡來的？）

你收到帳單，應該不是帳單自己走到你這兒來，若不是有人送來給你，就是郵寄來的，不管帳單怎麼到你的手中，帳單還是從別的地方來到你這裡，所以帳單也是 come（來到）你這裡。

◆ The bill has come at a bad time.
（帳單來的不是時候。）

你到店裡買東西，店員算了一下你買的東西之後，他會跟你說你買的東西總數是多少，也就是說這些東西的價錢加起來 comes to（達到）多少錢。

◆ Your grocery bill comes to $50.00.
（你買的雜貨總共是五十元。）

有人跟瑪麗說，你大學聯考落榜了，瑪麗一聽就昏了過去，大家趕快要搖醒她，搖了一會兒，瑪麗總算甦醒了，旁人看了，鬆了一口氣說，**Oh good, now she** comes **to.**，因為她被嚇走的三魂七魄又 comes to 她了嘛！

- Look, John comes to.
  （看，約翰甦醒了。）

某家店，某一樣式的洋裝，有好幾種不同的顏色可以挑選，也就是說，廠商送進來好幾種不同顏色的這一式洋裝；某一家鞋店，某一樣式的鞋子，有好幾種不同的尺寸可以挑選，也是可以說廠商送來各種尺寸的這式鞋子，所以我們說這式洋裝 comes in many colors，同樣的這式鞋子也是 comes in many sizes。

- Does this dress come in other colors?
  （這件洋裝你們有別的顏色嗎？）

- Do those shoes come in my size?
  （那雙鞋子有我的尺寸嗎？）

- These shoes come in four sizes.
  （這雙鞋子有四種尺寸。）

Come on

● Come on. 這句話有好幾個意思,上游泳課,約翰不敢從跳板上跳水,同學在一旁鼓勵他說,Come on, you can do it.(來吧,你做得到的)。Come on, 可以用在你要鼓勵別人說「做吧,你可以做到的」。

● 如果有人打電話給你說,你中獎了,得了頭獎五百萬,但是,你得先匯款 20 萬來,繳稅金,你才可以拿到你的獎金,就跟他說這句話吧,Oh come on, you can't fool me.(得了,我不會被騙的),不管對方是存心想訛詐你,或是在跟你開玩笑的騙你,你不要輕易上當,跟他說 Oh come on,(得了,你以為我那麼好騙啊)。

● 大伙兒要搭飛機去度假,眼看著搭飛機的時間快來不及了,約翰還慢條斯理的對著鏡子整理他的頭髮,大家簡直急昏了,趕快催他說,Come on, we're going to miss the plane.(快點,我們會趕不上飛機)。當你要催對方時,也可以跟他說 Come on,(來吧,快一點吧。)

How come?
（為什麼？）

● 在一個宴會上，大家正玩得高興，瑪麗突然說她要回家了，你忍不住就問她 How come?，約翰說他要去看醫生，你也可以問他 How come?，不過這樣問可有點 silly（傻問題），因為約翰當然是生病了才要去看醫生嗎？

● How come? 是一句口語，是問「為什麼」，與 why 的意思一樣。

12

cut
[kʌt]

基本上，用刀子切的英語就是 cut，刀子可以 cut（切）蛋糕、水果；剪刀可以 cut（剪）頭髮；割草機可以 cut（割）草。你如果不小心，刀子還會 cut（割傷）你。

若是把開銷減低或是減薪，就好像是用刀把開銷或是薪水給切短，所以也是把開銷或是薪水給 cut 了。

動詞三態 cut, cut, cut

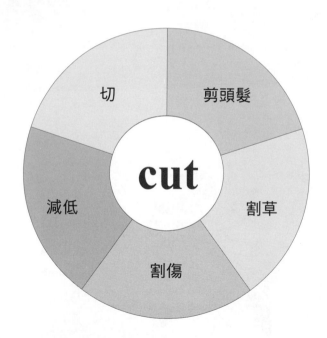

切

* The birthday girl is cutting the cake.
  （壽星在切蛋糕了。）

剪頭髮

* Where do you have your hair cut?
  （你都在哪裡剪頭髮？）

* You should have your hair cut
  already.
  （你應該剪頭髮了。）

割草

* John will cut the grass this afternoon.
  （約翰今天下午要割草。）

割傷

* John cut his chin when he shaved.
  （約翰刮鬍子的時候，割傷他的下巴。）

減低

* The company will lay off two hundred people to cut the cost.
  （公司要裁員兩百人，以減低開銷。）

* His salary was cut by 20%.
  （他被減薪百分之二十。）

cut 輕鬆學

☑ If Mary keeps cutting classes, she'll fail the course.

如果瑪莉繼續蹺課的話，她那一科一定會不及格。

☑ Don't cut corners. Let's do the job right.

不要偷工減料。我們把事情做好。

☑ The doctor told John to cut down on Coke.

醫生要約翰少喝可樂。

☑ He cut himself shaving.

他刮鬍子的時候，割傷他自己。

☑ I cut a piece of birthday cake for them all.

我給他們每人都切了一片生日蛋糕。

每天五分鐘

⏱ cut class 就是「蹺課」的意思。

⏱ cut corners 就是「偷工減料」。

⏱ cut down on 某樣東西，就是「減少使用某樣東西」或「減少吃某樣東西」的意思。

⏱ cut 是割傷，cut 的過去式也是 cut，如果句子是用過去式，主詞雖然是第三人稱單數也不加 s。

⏱ 用刀子切割東西就是 cut。

⏱ 切生日蛋糕就是 cut a birtyday cake。

 這句話英語怎麼說

☛ 你要寫字,發現忘了帶筆,你問朋友說,你有帶筆嗎?這句話英語怎麼說?

☛ 你到一家商店,要問他們有沒有賣化妝品,這句話英語怎麼說?

☛ 大家到公園玩,有幾個小朋友抓到一隻兔子,你說,他們抓到了一隻兔子,這句話英語怎麼說?

☛ 冬天到了,你又感冒了,你說,我每年冬天都感冒,這句話英語怎麼說?

這句話英語怎麼說

* 你有帶筆嗎?　　　　　　Do you carry a pen?

* 你們有賣化妝品嗎?　　　Do you carry make-up?

* 他們抓到了一隻兔子。　　They caught a rabbit.

* 我每年冬天都感冒。　　　I catch a cold every winter.

13

drop
[drɑp]

有東西從高處掉下去，就是那樣東西從高處 drop，而如果你手上拿著東西，一沒拿好，那樣東西也會 drop（掉下去）的。

大家在聊天，講到一個你不喜歡的話題，你要求大家別講了，也就要求大家停掉這個話題，把一個話題停掉，雖然不是像水果從樹上掉下來，或是球從你手上掉下去那樣有實質的東西往下掉，但是，話題停掉，也可以說是 drop 這話題，好像讓一個話題掉下去一樣，大家就別再談了。同樣的，如果你工作太累了，朋友也會建議你，把一切 drop，去度個假吧，別管工作或一切煩惱，也就好像讓這一切都從你腦子裡掉下去，不要放在你的腦子裡。

中文說「把說話聲音降低」、「股市下跌」、「雨勢、風勢下降」、「價錢下跌」、「失業率下降」，這些雖都不是實質的有東西從上往下掉，可也都是抽象的「下跌、下降」，所以英語都是用 drop 這個字。

掉下來　停止、結束

停止上某一門課　**drop**　降低（聲音、價錢、氣溫）

載某人到某個地方　風勢減弱

動詞三態　drop, dropped, dropped

精選例句

掉下來

* Ripe fruit dropped from the trees.
（熟的水果從樹上掉下來。）

* He dropped his pen.
（他的筆掉到地上。）

* Mary accidentally dropped her plant from the window.
（瑪莉不小心把她的花從窗戶掉下去。）

* I must have dropped my keys in the bus this morning.
（我的鑰匙一定是今早掉在公車上。）

停止、結束

* Let's drop the subject.
（我們不要談這個話題。）

* You should drop everything and take a vacation.
（你應該放下一切，去度假。）

降低
（聲音、價錢、氣溫）

* They dropped their voices as they went into the library.
（他們進了圖書館，就把聲音放低。）

* The temperature will drop below zero tonight.
（今晚氣溫會降到零下。）

* The stock market dropped today.
（今天股市下跌。）

* House prices have dropped sharply lately.
（最近房價跌得很厲害。）

* The unemployment rate has dropped.
（失業率已經下降。）

風勢減弱　* The wind speed has dropped.
（風勢已減弱。）

載某人到某個地方　* Could you drop me off at my house?
（你可以載我到我家嗎？）

停止上某一門課　* I wish I hadn't dropped piano lessons.
（我希望我沒有停掉鋼琴課。）

drop out
輟學

■ She dropped out of school.
（她輟學了。）

大家來說英語

drop by

● 如果你沒有什麼特別的事情,只是到朋友家坐坐串門子,英語有三種說法,就是:drop by, drop in 和 drop over。

● 請朋友有空到你家來坐坐,可以說 Drop in sometime., Drop by sometime. 或 Drop over sometime. 你也可以邀請朋友說 Drop by for a drink. 或是 Please drop in when you get a chance. (你有空,就過來坐坐。)

● 對外地的朋友,你可以跟他說 Drop by whenever you are in the town. (你到本市來的時候,要過來坐坐。)

● 以下這句話,可是誠心十足,歡迎之意更甚,We would love you to drop over some time. (我們喜歡你有空過來坐坐。)

drop me a note
(捎一封信給我)

● 當有朋友要遠行時,你會叫他,記得跟你寫信,以便保持聯繫,英語的說法就是,Drop me a note. 或 Drop me a line. 或是 Drop me a note when you get there. (你到的時候,給我寫封信。)

14

fail
[fel]

所有要做的事情失敗了，英語就是 fail；如果考試考了不及格，當然也算是 fail 了，應該要去做的事情沒去做，就是 fail to 做這件事，而機器故障就是這個機器 fail 了，農作物欠收更可以說是收成 fail。

動詞三態 fail, failed, failed

精選例句

失敗

＊ Peace talks between the two countries have failed.

（兩國之間的和平談判失敗。）

＊ Millions of people have tried to lose weight and failed.

（已經有幾百萬人嘗試減肥卻失敗。）

生意失敗

＊ Several banks failed during the recession.

（很多家銀行在不景氣時倒閉。）

考試不及格	* If you don't study hard, you'll fail the exam. （如果你不用功讀書，你會考不及格。）
	* He failed the driving test the first time he took it. （他第一次考路考的時候，沒考過。）
沒有做應該做的事	* John failed to take the final exam. （約翰沒有去考期末考。）
	* She failed to do the dishes for five days in a row. （她一連五天沒有洗碗。）
	* His parachute failed to open. （他的降落傘沒有張開。）
	* My grandchildren never fail to phone me on my birthday. （我生日那一天，我的孫子們從沒有忘記打電話給我。）
機器故障	* The rocket's engine failed a few seconds after take-off. （火箭的引擎在發射後幾秒鐘就發生故障。）
農作物歉收	* The entire Idaho potato crop failed miserably this year. （整個愛達荷州的馬鈴薯今年嚴重的歉收。）

15

fall
[fɔl]

樹葉從樹上掉到地上，書本從書架上掉到地上，小孩子從腳踏車上掉下來，或是小孩子掉到河裡去，甚至於下雨、下雪都是 fall，以上這些「fall」都是有實質的東西從高處往下掉。其他非實質東西的往下掉，例如：溫度、價格、利息等的下跌都是 fall。

動詞三態 fall, fell, fallen

掉落

跌倒

城市、陣地被攻破

fall

跌下來

政府垮台

溫度、價格等下跌

掉落

* The leaves have started falling again.
（樹葉又開始掉了。）

* Apples fell from the tree.
（蘋果從樹上掉下來。）

* Mary fell down the stairs and broke her leg.
（瑪莉從樓梯上摔下來，摔斷腿。）

* He fell into a lake.
（他掉進湖裡。）

* The weather report says snow will fall tonight.
（氣象報告說今晚會下雪。）

跌倒

* She fell and hit her head.
（她跌倒，碰到頭。）

跌下來

* She fell off the bike and broke her arm.
（她從腳踏車上跌下來，摔斷手臂。）

溫度、 價格等 下跌	* In winter the temperature often falls below zero. （冬天時，氣溫常降到零下。） * Interest rates fell sharply. （利息突然下降。） * House prices are falling. （屋價在下跌。） * The price of gas has fallen by one dollar. （油價已經下跌一塊錢。）
政府垮台	* The government fell and was re-placed by another. （這個政府垮台，被其他人取代。）
城市、 陣地 被攻破	* The city fell after a long battle. （在久戰之後，該城市被攻破。）

fall 輕鬆學

☑ I fell asleep while watching the movie.
　　我看電影時睡著了。

☑ The club I belonged to fell apart.
　　我參加的社團解散了。

☑ John fell in love with Mary.
　　約翰愛上瑪莉。

☑ John fell off the bike and broke his arm.
　　約翰從腳踏車上摔下來，摔斷手臂。

每天五分鐘

🕐 fall asleep 是片語，意思是「睡著了」。

🕐 fall apart 是片語，意思是「解散掉」。

🕐 約翰 falls in love with 瑪麗，就是「約翰愛上瑪麗」。

🕐 fall off something 就是「從某個地方摔下來」。

16

find
[faɪnd]

你找到某樣東西，就是 find 那樣東西；若是要想辦法挪出時間來，就是想辦法 find 時間；若是你要到某個地方去，要找路就是要 find the way to 那個地方；若是你要去上課，到了教室才發現那堂課取消了，你要去上課之前並不知道，到了教室才知道，也就是到了教室才 find 課被取消這個事實。

動詞三態 find, found, found

找到   **find**   發現

精選例句

找到

* I hope we can find a parking lot.
（我希望我們找得到停車的地方。）

* Could you find me a nice second-hand car?
（你能不能替我找一部好的二手車？）

* We found the solution to this problem.
（我們找到解決這個問題的方法。）

* Will we ever find a cure for cancer?
（我們找得到治療癌症的方法嗎？）

* We found a really good restaurant near the hotel.
（我們在旅館附近找到一家很好的餐廳。）

* I wouldn't mind helping you, but I can't find the time right now.
（我不介意幫你的忙，但是我現在沒時間。）

* Will you be able to find your way to my office?
（到我辦公室的路，你找得到嗎？）

發現

* When I got to the classroom, I found that class was cancelled.
（我到教室的時候，才發現該堂課取消了。）

* She finds that she can lose weight just by eating less.
（她發現只要少吃點，她的體重就可以減輕。）

find out

發現

■ I just found out our library books are overdue.
（我剛發現我們跟圖書館借的書過期了。）

17

go
[go]

go 這個字就是「從一個地方到另一個地方」，你可以 go home（回家），go to school（去上學），go to Hong Kong（去香港）。

go 也有從一個地方離開的意思，天晚了，你說「我該走了」，就是你要離開那個地方，下課了，學生都走了，也就是學生都離開教室。

動詞三態 go, went, gone

精選例句

走、去

* It's late. I must be going.
（天晚了，我該走了。）

* The teacher hasn't gone yet.
（老師還沒有離開。）

* I wanted to go, but Mary wanted to stay.
（我想要走，但是瑪莉想要留下來。）

* I'll just go and get my coat.
（我就去拿我的大衣。）

* Shall we go get something to eat?
（我們去吃點東西好嗎？）

* John has gone to Hong Kong.
（約翰已經到香港去了。）

* Where are you going?
（你要去哪裡？）

* We're going to my parents' house for New Year.

（我們要去我父母家過新年。）

* What time are you going to the airport?

（你什麼時候要去機場？）

* They all went away and left me alone.

（他們都走了，留下我一個人。）

* Can we go home?

（我們回家好嗎？）

* John is too young to go to school.

（約翰還太小，不能去上學。）

go	swimming（去游泳）	fishing（去釣魚）
	jogging（去慢跑）	skiing（去滑雪）

■ John has gone skiing in Aspen.

（約翰已經到艾斯本滑雪去了。）

go （變成；成為）	wild（玩野了）	bad（變壞了）
	sour（變酸了）	down（下跌）
	crazy（瘋了）	wrong（出差錯）

🔄 一到放假，大人們最怕小孩子 go wild（玩野）了，小孩子一旦 go wild，假期一過，心收不回來，可就難辦了。

◆ After the summer vacation, the children went wild.
（過了暑假，孩子們都玩野了。）

🔄 吃早餐時，你喝了一口牛奶，發現牛奶酸酸的，你知道牛奶 go bad（壞了）或 go sour（變酸了）。

◆ The milk went sour.
（牛奶變酸了。）

從事貿易的企業界人士最注意美元的升貶了，出口商一遇到美元 go down（貶值）可是叫苦連天啊。

◆ The value of the dollar is going down.
（美元在貶值。）

刮颱風天，你的朋友說要到海邊去看颱風颳起驚濤駭浪的景致，你肯定要罵他，你真是 go crazy（瘋了）。

◆ I think you're going crazy.
（我認為你是瘋了。）

大夥兒精心策劃的計畫失敗了，大家要趕緊檢討什麼地方 go wrong（出了差錯）。

◆ Our plans failed. I don't know what went wrong.
（我們的計畫失敗。我不知道出了什麼差錯。）

你聽到同事瑪麗說她的頭很痛，隔天你再遇到她時，可得關心的問一聲，你頭痛（headahce）好了嗎？這句話英語很簡單，go 這個字就可以做「痛楚消失了」的意思。

◆ Has your headache gone yet?
（你頭痛好了嗎？）

go 這個字可以做「東西不見了」的意思，你要看電視，卻四處找不到遙控器，為了希望家裡其他人知道你找不到遙控器，你可以大聲嚷道 The remote control is gone.，希望你家那些愛管閒事的小蘿蔔頭們會來幫你找。

◆ The TV remote control is gone.
（電視遙控器不見了。）

又是秋風起，紅葉滿天的時節，你說時間是不是過得真快，這「時間過去了」的英語就是 go，我真不知道我們有沒有機會說這句 Time goes slowly.（時間過得真慢。）

◆ The summer is going fast.
（今年夏天過的真快。）

◆ Time goes quickly when you're busy.
（當你忙碌的時候，時間過得很快。）

時間飛速的過去，我們的體力也一天天衰退，視力 is starting to go（開始減弱），聽力也 is going（漸漸衰退），最終，我們也要 go（死）的。

- ◆ My sight is starting to go.
  （我的視力開始變差。）

- ◆ My hearing is going.
  （我的聽力漸漸衰退。）

- ◆ His parents are all gone. He is on his own.
  （他的雙親都已過世。他要靠他自己。）

人走了是 go，東西漸漸變弱，終究消耗掉不能用，也是 go，例如：燈泡壞了，電池沒電了。

- ◆ The bulb in the kitchen is gone.
  （廚房的燈泡壞了。）

你昨天才給你太太一萬塊，今天她又伸手跟你要錢，你忍不住要問她，Where did all the money I gave you go?（我給你的錢都到哪裡去了），這時，當太太的也不能示弱，你可以告訴他，你知道嗎，這年頭，一萬塊錢 doesn't go far（可買不到什麼東西）。

- ◆ Where did all the money I gave you go?
  （我給你的錢都到哪裡去了？）

- ◆ Two hundred dollars doesn't go far these days.
  （這年頭，兩百元買不到什麼東西。）

go 輕鬆學

☑ We went by plane. 　　　我們搭飛機前往。

☑ I'll go by bus. 　　　我要坐公車去。

☑ Are you going by train? 　你要搭火車去嗎？

☑ Do green shirt and blue pants go together?
　　　　　　綠色的襯衫和藍色的褲子配起來好看嗎？

☑ Does this tie go well with my shirt?
　　　　　　　　這條領帶配我的襯衫好看嗎？

☑ Let's go for a walk after lunch.
　　　　　　　　　　吃過午飯我們去散步。

☑ Do you want to go to the movies?
　　　　　　　　　　　你要去看電影嗎？

！ 每天五分鐘

⏱ 搭乘某樣交通工具去某個地方，英語的成語就「go by ＋ 搭乘的交通工具」，例如：go by plane，go by bus，go by train。

⏱ 如果兩個顏色 go together，表示「這兩個顏色搭配起來很好看」。

⏱ 如果某件東西 go with 另一樣東西，表示「這兩樣東西配起來很好看。」

⏱ 去散步的英語是 go for a walk：去游泳的英語是 go for a swim.，去慢跑的英語是 go for a jog。

○○○○○ 大家來說英語 ○○○○●

What do you go by?

● 我在美國上課，尤其是第一堂課，有時教授點名時會順口問學生 What do you go by? 美國學生就會馬上給老師一個名字，老師就記在他的點名簿上，有時學生會回答說，就是你剛剛叫的那個名字，如果老美教授問到中國學生 What do you go by? 中國學生不是來個相應不理，就是一臉茫然，對教授相應不理的學生其實根本不曉得老師在問他問題，知道老師在問他問題的學生，卻因不曉得老師在問他什麼，而一臉茫然。這句話到底是什麼意思呢？原來美國名字，常有別的暱稱，例如：名叫 Elizabeth 的女孩，她的同學多半會叫她 Lisa；名叫 Robert 的男生，他的同學多半會叫他 Bob。有時學生自己不喜歡你叫他正式的名字，他會告訴你他 go by 另外一個名字，也就是說，他喜歡你平常叫他那個名字。所以，教授有時會問學生 What do you go by? 你希望我點名時怎麼叫你？尤其是中國學生的名字，對老美來說很難念，有時中國學生就會取個美國名字，讓老美好記又好念，所以，教授在叫了中國學生的正式名字之後，常喜歡問 What do you go by? 老美教授想問你，有沒有另一個比較好念的名字，他平常叫你那個名字就好。

大家來說英語

For here or to go?
（內用還是外帶？）

- 你如果到美國的速食餐廳買食物，櫃臺小姐一定先問你要內用還是外帶？這句話的英語就是 For here or to go?

Here she goes again.
（她又這麼做了）

- Here she goes again. 就是說某人常愛做一些令你討厭的事情，當她又這麼做時，你不禁要嘀咕道，Here she goes again.

- 你們公司有個女同事，平常就喜歡抱怨公司的主管對她不好，抱怨她的工作太多，總之，就是有一大堆事情好抱怨的，現在她又在抱怨，其他的同事都不做事，事情全是她一個人在做，別人聽了，真煩，不禁低聲說 Here she goes again.

 這句話英語怎麼說

☛ 你如果遇到熟人,要問他一切可好,用 go 這個字,這句話英語怎麼說?

☛ 你知道約翰去開會,開會完後,你問他,會議開得如何,用 go 這個字,這句話英語怎麼說?

☛ 你開完會,同事問你,會議開得怎麼樣,你說,今天會議開得很順利,用 go 這個字,這句話英語怎麼說?

☛ 你的棒球隊有校際比賽,結果你的隊伍打得不好,同學問你比賽的情況,你說,我們隊球賽打得不好,用 go 這個字,這句話英語怎麼說?

☛ 一早起來,你要開車去上班,車子卻發不動,你進屋裡頭去跟太太說,我們的車子發不動,用 go 這個字,這句話英語怎麼說?

☛ 你的老爺車一天到晚出毛病,你說,那部車子一定要賣掉才行,也就是說,你一定要那部車走,用 go 這個字,這句話英語怎麼說?

這句話英語怎麼說

* 你一切都好吧? How's it going?

* 會議開得如何啊? How did the meeting go?

* 今天會議開得很順利。 The meeting went well today.

* 我們隊球賽打得不好。 The game don't go well for our team.

* 我們的車子發不動。 Our car won't go.

* 這部車子一定要賣掉才行。 The car must go.

18

get
[gɛt]

get 的過去式和過去分詞是 got，有人給你東西，你收到了，就是你 got 那樣東西。有時你得到某樣東西不是人家給你的，而是你自己花錢去買的，你也是 got（得到）了那樣東西。

如果你花時間去讀書，也可以 got（得到）一個學位。

動詞三態 get, got, got

問問題

精選例句

* What did you get for your birthday?
（你生日時收到什麼生日禮物？）

* I got a letter from Mary this morning.
（我今早收到瑪麗來的信。）

買到

* Where did you get that dress?
（你在哪裡買到那件洋裝？）

有

* What kind of car has your brother got?
（你哥哥開什麼樣的車子？）

* John's got a Master's Degree in History.
（約翰擁有歷史學的碩士學位。）

你過生日時，令尊送你一部電腦做生日禮物，過完了生日，你可以很驕傲的跟你的朋友說，我生日時 got（得到）一部電腦。

◆ I got a computer for my birthday.
（我收到一部電腦做我的生日禮物。）

大夥兒商量要去海濱玩，你是個很實際的人，第一個想到的問題當然是 get to the beach（到海邊）要多久啊？

◆ How long will it take to get to the beach?
（到海邊要多久？）

↻ 大家的開心果約翰又在講笑話，搞得整屋子人笑彎了腰，只有瑪麗一臉茫然，你知道從小在美國受教育的瑪麗一定是聽不懂約翰的笑話，你趕緊問她，**Did you get the joke?**，聽懂別人的意思，英語就是 get 這個字。當然，瑪麗是聽不懂約翰的笑話，她就會回答你說 I didn't get it.（我沒聽懂。）

◆ **Did you get the joke?**
（你聽得懂這個笑話嗎？）

注意到　　＊ **Did you get the look on his face?**
（你有沒有注意到他臉上的表情？）

聽到　　＊ **When Mary got the news, she passed out.**
（當瑪莉聽到這個消息的時候，她就昏倒。）

get ＋ 形容詞	
lost（迷路）	hot（越來越熱）
angry（生氣）	married（結婚）
late（天晚了）	wet（濕了）
cold（涼了）	ridiculous（越來越荒唐）

↻ 你們幾個好朋友一起到溪頭去玩，瑪麗和約翰說要出去走一走，很晚了，他們兩個還不回來，有人開始擔心他們，你知道他們兩個一定是談心談得不知今夕是何夕，忘了回來，但是，你總得給他們留個面子吧，你就說 They must get lost.

◆ **They must get lost.**
（他們一定是迷路了。）

好不容易，瑪麗和約翰終於回來了，大夥兒可不信你說的他們迷路了，定要約翰交代清楚，他們到哪兒去了，害得大家擔心，約翰開頭是笑而不答，被大家逼急了，可有點要惱羞成怒的樣子了，總該有人出來打圓場吧，說饒了他吧，你們看 He is getting angry.

◆ He is getting angry.
（他生氣了。）

◆ It's getting dark.
（天色漸漸黑了。）

◆ Eat your dinner before it gets cold.
（飯冷之前快吃。）

◆ It's getting hot in here.
（這裡面越來越熱。）

◆ John and Mary are getting married in June.
（約翰和瑪麗六月要結婚。）

◆ Get out of the rain or you'll get wet.
（不要待在雨中，否則你會淋濕。）

◆ This is getting ridiculous.
（這越來越荒唐。）

get 輕鬆學

☐ What time do you usually get up?
你通常都幾點起床？

☐ Get on the bus.
上車吧。

☐ I got a busy signal.
對方電話有人在使用。

☐ He just didn't get it.
他就是聽不懂。

☐ It's good to see you, Mary. We'll have to get together again.
瑪莉，很高興見到你。我們應該再聚一聚。

！每天五分鐘

⏱ get up 是個片語，是「起床」的意思。

⏱ get on 這個片語，是「上車」的意思。

⏱ 打電話時，如果對方電話正在使用，你就會聽到「使用中 (busy)」的信號。

⏱ 聽不懂別人說的笑話。

⏱ get together 這個片語，是「朋友相聚」的意思。

大家來說英語

Get lost!
（走開，別煩我！）

● 大家一定學過 get lost 這個片語是「迷路」的意思。Get lost! 這句話還有別的意思，例如：有一個男孩子喜歡妳，所以一天到晚就對妳跟前跟後的，妳實在煩到不行，現在他又在妳眼前出現了，邀妳今晚跟他去看電影，妳就可以大聲的叫他 Get lost。在這裡 Get lost！的意思就是叫對方走開，消失到別的地方去吧，別在妳的面前出現。

Get out of here.
（別油嘴滑舌的！）

● 如果我問你 Get out of here. 是什麼意思，你一定回答是叫對方「離開」或是語氣更重一點，叫對方「滾開」的意思。可是，你有沒有看過美國電視劇「黃金女郎」，有一晚有一位男士來到三個黃金女郎的家裡，這位男士看到劇裡的風騷女郎布蘭琪時，對布蘭琪說，妳好漂亮，只見布蘭琪笑得天花亂墜，又微嗔的說道 Get out of here.，你說布蘭琪是要叫那位男士離開還是滾開呢，都不是，Get out of here. 在這裡是「去去去，別油嘴滑舌的，吃老娘豆腐」的意思。

19

give
[gɪv]

拿某樣東西給某人的英語就是 give。

give 也可以做「提供某樣東西給某人」的意思，例如：載約翰去上學，就是 give him a ride，幫約翰一個忙就是 give him a hand。

有時別人給的東西，並不是你要的，但是，你卻不能夠不接受，例如：老師 give 學生許多家庭作業，老闆 give 他的員工很多工作，公司的電腦系統都可能 give 你麻煩。

我們說噪音讓我的頭很痛，英語的說法就是噪音 gives me a headache.

替某人辦個宴會，我們可以說是 give 她一個宴會。

動詞三態 give, gave, given

給；供給

精選例句

* What did John give you for your birthday?
（約翰給你什麼生日禮物？）

* Give the rabbit some carrots.
（給那隻兔子一些紅蘿蔔。）

* Can you give me a ride to school?
（你可以載我去學校嗎？）

* I'll give you a call tonight.
（我今晚會打個電話給你。）

* My English teacher gave us a lot of homework today.
（今天我的英文老師給我們許多功課。）

* My boss is always giving me a hard time these days.
（我老闆最近老是找我的麻煩。）

* This new computer system is giving us a lot of trouble.
（這個新的電腦系統給我們很多麻煩。）

* The noise gave me a real headache.
（那噪音讓我頭很痛。）

* The doctor gave him something for the pain.
（醫生給他一些止痛的藥。）

給予幫忙 * Can you give me a hand?

（你可以幫我一個忙嗎？）

舉辦宴會 * We are giving Mary a wedding shower Sunday afternoon.

（星期天下午我們要為瑪莉舉辦一個結婚送禮會。）

give 除了是實際上拿東西給對方之外，當你給對方任何東西，包括資訊、指示，意見甚至於你答應對方的話，都是用 give。

你付錢買東西，你也是 give 錢給對方，然後把東西買過來。

有些事情要做需要時間，所以，要做這些事情，你需要 give 對方時間去做。

提供消息、資訊

* The first chapter gives a broad outline of the book.

（第一篇大概說明了這本書的大綱。）

* Can you give me some information on buying a new car?

（你能不能在買新車方面給我一些意見？）

* I gave Mary my word that I'd take her to the movies.

（我已經答應瑪莉，我要帶她去看電影。）

容許

* You should give yourself an hour to drive to the airport.

（你要開到機場，需要給你自己一小時的時間。）

* Give him time. It's always hard to learn another language.

（給他一些時間，學外國語言總是困難的。）

* I'll give you another chance to make up.

（我再給你一次機會補救。）

付

* I'll give you $5000 for your old car.
（你那部舊車我想用五千元來買。）

* GE's bond gives a good return of ten percent a year.
（GE 公司的債券一年有百分之十的好回收。）

傳染疾病

* Don't come too close. I don't want to give you my cold.
（不要太靠近我。我不想傳染感冒給你。）

因為外力的推動而移動

* I tried to move the box, but it wouldn't give an inch.
（我想要推動這個盒子，但是完全推不動。）

法院的判決

* He was given two years.
（他被判處兩年的徒刑。）

約翰和瑪麗要結婚了,可是你對他們的婚姻卻不看好,所以,你就會帶點幸災樂禍的口氣說,對他們的婚姻,I give it two months. 意思就是你估計他們的婚姻只能維持兩個月。

- ◆ John and Susan are going to get married?
  I give it two months.
  (約翰和蘇珊要結婚?我估計這婚姻只能維持兩個月。)

如果某種材料 gives,那就是說你若加壓力,它就會彎曲或延伸。

- ◆ The leather will give a little after you've worn the shoes a while.
  (這雙鞋子你穿了一段時間之後,皮革就會軟一點。)

give 輕鬆學

☑ The doctor asked him to give up smoking.

醫生要他戒煙。

☑ Don't give up.

別放棄。

☑ I'm the one who always gives in.

我每次都是屈服。

☑ Why do I have to give in to you?

我為什麼要屈服於你？

☑ She gave birth to a baby boy.

她生了一個男孩。

每天五分鐘

⏱ give up something 就是「停止做某件事情」的意思。

⏱ give up 就是「放棄」的意思。

⏱ give in 就是「屈服」的意思。

⏱ give into 某人就是「屈服於某人」的意思。

⏱ give birth to 就是「生小孩」的意思。

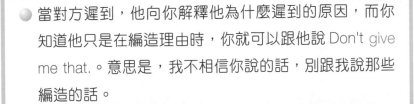

大家來說英語

Don't give me that.
（別給我編故事。）

● 當對方遲到，他向你解釋他為什麼遲到的原因，而你知道他只是在編造理由時，你就可以跟他說 Don't give me that.。意思是，我不相信你說的話，別跟我說那些編造的話。

Give me five!

● 還記得電影「魔鬼終結者第二集」這部電影裡，阿諾飾演的機器人要救的那個小孩，他喜歡教阿諾所不知道的人類的行為和思想，有一次，他把手掌伸出來面向阿諾，跟阿諾說 Give me five!，教阿諾也把手伸出來跟他對掌一拍，這是美國年輕人互相打招呼的玩意兒，你的手掌張開伸出時，不是有五個手指頭嗎，要跟對方拍掌打招呼，就把手伸出來，手掌張開面向對方，說 Give me five. 對方也就會把手掌張開伸出來跟你一擊掌，彼此就這樣互相打一下招呼。

20

have
[hæv]

have 可以是擁有實質的東西，例如：車子、書、玩具、姊妹等，也可以是 have 抽象的東西，例如：有問題、主意等或是在宴會上玩得很快樂，英語說 have a good time。

動詞三態 have, had, had

精選例句

有

* How many cars do you have?
（你有幾部車子？）

* Do you have any questions?
（你有問題嗎？）

* We had a good time at Mary's party.
（我們在瑪莉的宴會玩得很愉快。）

* She has blonde hair and blue eyes.
（她有金黃色的頭髮，藍色的眼睛。）

請求幫忙	* How many pages does the book have? （這本書有幾頁？） * She has an idea on how to make the plan work. （要如何使這個計畫作得成，她有一個主意。）
生病	* I had a cold. （我感冒了。） * My brother might have the chicken pox. （我弟弟可能是在長水痘。）
have 當 使役動詞	* I had my house painted last week. （上星期我叫人把房子油漆過。） * Where do you usually have your hair cut? （你通常在哪裡剪頭髮？）
吃；喝	* She sat down and had another drink. （她坐下來，並且再喝一杯。） * We usually have dinner at 7:00. （我們通常在七點吃晚飯。）
想要某樣 飲料或點 心	* I'll have the apple pie for dessert, please. （我的點心要蘋果派。） * I'll have coffee. （我要咖啡。）

have 輕鬆學

☐ I had a cold.

我感冒了。

☐ John has a crush on Mary.

約翰愛上瑪莉。

☐ Mary, can I have a word with you?

瑪莉，我可以私下跟你談談嗎？

☐ We have to do homework everyday.

我們每天都必須寫功課。

☐ John had a fit when he found his car had been damaged.

當約翰發現他的車子被撞壞時，他很生氣。

每天五分鐘

- have a cold 是「感冒」的意思。

- 約翰 has a crush on 瑪麗，就是約翰「愛上」瑪麗。

- have a word with 某人，就是找某人私下談一談，這裡含有要找他談正事的意思，而不是要找他聊聊天。

- have to 是「必須」的意思。

- have a fit 就是「很生氣」的意思。

●●●● 大家來說英語 ●●●●

I have cold feet.
（我感到害怕。）

● 有人在結婚前突然說他不想結婚了，朋友就說他 has cold feet。某人 has cold feet. 這句話的意思就是對於某件他要做的事情，感到害怕。

● 例如：你原本要在畢業典禮祝詞，到畢業典禮之前，你感到害怕不願意上台去祝詞，你說 I can't give my speech now. I have cold feet.（我現在沒辦法祝詞。我害怕。）

Do you have to......?
（你非得這樣做不可以嗎？）

● have to 是「必須」的意思，問人家 Do you have to 做某件事？這句話不是在關心對方，是不是一定要去做一件事，這句話是含有抗議的意思，是你對他正在做的事情表示不滿，而問他，你一定要這麼做嗎，你可以停了吧？例如：你住在學校宿舍裡，明天你有一個很重要的考試，你正緊張的在 K 書，你的室友卻拿著電話，大聲的講個不停，你實在忍無可忍，只好跟他說 Do you have to speak so loud?（你非得講那麼大聲不可以嗎？講小聲一點好嗎？）

21

hear
[hɪr]

hear 的功能就是人的五官之一，就是耳朵聽得見聲音的功能。除了聽到聲音之外，對方說的話，你聽得懂，也是 hear，你要告訴對方，我懂你說的話，就是 I hear what you are saying。

聽到一些消息，也是用耳朵 hear 到的，甚至於法官審理案件也要用耳朵聽，所以審理案件的英語也是 hear。

動詞三態 hear, heard, heard

問問題

精選例句

* Did you hear that strange noise?
  （你有沒有聽到那奇怪的噪音？）

* My grandmother doesn't hear well.
  （我的祖母聽不太清楚。）

* Did you hear the baby crying?
  （你有沒有聽到嬰孩在哭？）

* She faintly heard the telephone ringing in the kitchen.
  （她微微聽到廚房裡電話鈴響著。）

* I heard him walking down the stairs.
  （我聽到他走下樓。）

* I'm sorry, I didn't hear what you said.

（對不起，我沒聽到你說什麼。）

hear	聽懂別人的意思
	有人告訴你一些事情
	聽說
	審理案子

聽懂別人的意思

* I hear what you are saying, but I disagree.

（我懂得你的意思，但是我不同意。）

有人告訴你一些事情

* I'm sorry to hear that.

（聽到那件事，我很難過。）

* I'm glad to hear that you are getting better.

（聽到你好多了，我很高興。）

聽說

* I hear you're quitting the job.
（我聽說你要辭職。）

* I hear prices are going up.
（我聽說價錢上漲了。）

* I heard that John was fired.
（我聽說約翰被開除。）

* Did you hear about the accident?
（你有沒有聽說那件車禍的消息？）

* I've heard a lot about you.
（我常常聽到你的事情。）

* Have you heard anything of John lately?
（你有沒有約翰最近的消息？）

審理案子

* The judge will hear the case on May 10th.
（法官五月十日要審理這個案子。）

hear 輕鬆學

☐ Did you hear what I said?
　　　　我說的話你聽到了嗎？

☐ Have you heard from John?
　　　　約翰有沒有跟你聯絡？

☐ Did you hear about Mary?
　　　　你聽說瑪莉的事嗎？

☐ What do you hear from your brother in America?
　　　　你哥哥在美國，寄信來說些什麼事？

☐ I've heard of John Lin, but I've never met him.
　　　　我聽過林約翰這個人，但是我從未見過他。

每天五分鐘

🕐 hear 可以做「聽到別人說話」的意思。

🕐 hear from 是個片語，是「收到消息」或「收到對方寄來的信」的意思。

🕐 hear about 是「得知某人發生的事」。

🕐 hear of someone 是「聽說過這個人」的意思。

大家來說英語

Do you hear me?

- 妳叫妳的兒子這個週末要把房間整理乾淨，只見他一邊聽著音樂，一邊搖頭晃腦的回答你，嗯嗯，妳也不知道他到底把妳的話聽進去了沒有，還是只是習慣性的答應著，實際上，根本沒有聽到你叫他整理房間的命令，此時，妳應該提高聲調對他喊道 Do you hear me?，一定要他很明確的回答你，他不僅聽到了，而且聽清楚妳的要求才行。

- Do you hear me? 這句口語，就是用在你要確定對方有聽到你說的話，而且也明白你在說什麼的時候，尤其是你在命令對方做什麼事情的時候。

94

I've heard so much about you.

 你的先生介紹他的同事約翰跟你認識,由於約翰跟你先生是在做同組工作,你先生平常就跟妳提過他的同事約翰,所以,當有機會妳先生介紹約翰跟你認識時,妳就可以跟約翰說 I've heard so much about you. 妳就是在跟約翰說,我先生常常跟我提到你。

 當約翰聽到這句話,可能會回答 All good, I hope.,這句話的意思就是說,我希望妳先生都是跟你說我的好話。

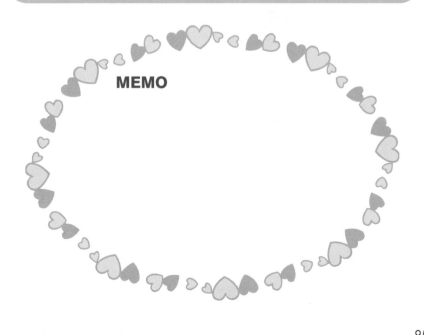

MEMO

22

hold
[hold]

hold 這個字就是「拿著」的意思,一對情侶手牽著手,也就是彼此 hold 對方的手。你如果是擔任某家公司的某個職位,那你就是 hold 這個職位。你如果手上握有某家公司的股份,你也就是 hold 這家公司的股份。而一間禮堂能夠 hold 多少人?那張椅子你坐下去,不會壞,就表示這張椅子可以 hold 得住你。

動詞三態　hold, held, held

拿著

* Can you hold the bags for me while I open the door?

（我開門的時候，你可不可以替我拿著袋子？）

* She held the baby in her arms.

（她抱著嬰孩在手上。）

* The couple held hands and sat at the beach.

（這一對情侶手牽著手坐在海邊。）

擔任某一重要的職位

* Most of the management positions are held by men.

（管理階層的職位大都是男士擔任。）

擁有、持有

* He holds 10,000 shares of the company.

（他擁有一萬股這個公司的股份。）

容納、包含

* The auditorium holds 2000 people.

（這座禮堂可容納兩千人。）

* This box will hold all of my stuff.

（這個盒子可以裝我所有的東西。）

支撐　　　* I don't think that chair will hold you.

（我不認為那個椅子能夠支撐你。）

如果你到圖書館要借書，卻發現忘了帶圖書證，你可以把你選好要借的書，交給圖書館管理員，請他幫你 hold 這些書，不要借出，你回家拿圖書證就來借。或是你到商店去買東西，卻發現錢不夠，你也可以請店員幫你把你要買的東西 hold 著，你回去拿錢再來買。如果你跟某家旅館預定了房間，他們就會為你 hold 一間房間。

◆ Will you hold "The Old Man and the Sea" for me?

（請你替我把『老人與海』一書留著。）

◆ They will hold a double room for us.

（他們會為我們留一間雙人房。）

hold 輕鬆學

☐ They are holding hands.

他們手牽著手。

☐ She was holding a large bag.

她手裡拿著一個大袋子。

☐ Hold your head up.

把頭抬起來。

☐ Hold on. I'll go get her.

請稍候，我去叫她來聽電話。

☐ How long can you hold your breath?

你能夠摒住呼吸多久？

每天五分鐘

🕐 hold hands 兩個人手牽著手。

🕐 hold 就是用手拿著。

🕐 Hold your head up. 叫對方「把頭抬起來」。

🕐 hold on 是個片語，叫對方「電話拿著，別掛斷」。

🕐 hold one's breath 是「摒住呼吸」的意思。

23

keep
[kip]

keep 是「保持一定狀態、不要變動」的意思，你如果決定把舊車留著，不把它賣掉就是 keep 這部舊車。

你如果有貴重的東西，就應該把它 keep 在一個安全的地方。

保守秘密就是 keep a secret，若是要讓肉保持新鮮，就是 keep the meat fresh。

動詞三態 keep, kept, kept

留著

* I kept $200 for myself and gave him $50.
（我自己留兩百元，給他五十元。）

* If you like the book, you can keep it.
（如果你喜歡這本書，你可以留著。）

* We want to keep the old car.
（這部舊車我們想要留著。）

保持、繼續

* Try to keep the balance.
（想辦法保持平衡。）

* He keeps telling me the same story.
（他一直告訴我同一個故事。）

* I don't know what's keeping him.
（我不知道什麼事絆住他。）

* She kept her trim figure.
（她保持苗條的身材。）

* The teacher asked the class to keep quiet.
（老師要求班上保持安靜。）

* Come closer to the fireplace. It'll keep you warm.

（來火爐邊，可以使你保持暖和。）

**把東西
放在
某個地方**

* She keeps her jewelry in a safe.

（她把她的珠寶放在保險櫃。）

* He keeps his money in a savings account.

（他的錢存在儲蓄帳號。）

* I always keep an umbrella in the car.

（我總是放一把傘在車上。）

使維持

* She kept a diary of what she did every day.

（她有一本日記，記她每天作的事。）

* Can I trust you to keep a secret?

（我可以信任你會守祕密嗎？）

* The refrigerator keeps meat fresh.

（冰箱使肉保持新鮮。）

keep 輕鬆學

☐ I hope we can keep in touch.

我希望我們能保持聯繫。

☐ I'll try not to keep you waiting.

我會盡量不讓你等。

☐ We all help my mother keep house.

我們都幫助媽媽整理屋子。

☐ I'll keep my word.

我會遵守諾言。

☐ Keep off the grass.

別踐踏草地。

每天五分鐘

🕐 keep in touch 是個片語，是「保持聯繫」的意思。

🕐 keep house 就是「照料、整理房子」的意思。

🕐 keep 某人的 word 就是「遵守諾言」的意思。

🕐 Keep off the grass. 這句話常常是公園裡草地旁的警告牌，
叫大家遠離草地，別踐踏草地。

Keep the change.
（不用找錢了）

● 乘坐計程車，如果車資是 98 元，你可以給計程車司機 100 塊錢，同時跟司機說 Keep the change.，就是跟司機說「不用找錢了」，就讓那兩塊錢當小費賞給司機。

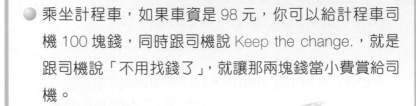

Keep your shirt on!
（別急，有耐心點。）

● 你跟妹妹要去逛街，她高興的很快就準備好了，可是你又要挑挑看要穿哪一件衣服，又要化妝，慢慢地來，你妹妹等不及了，一直催你快點，你就可以跟她說 Keep your shirt on!，叫她別急，有耐心點。

 **這句話英語怎麼說**

👉 約翰在講笑話，大家笑得不可開交，你看瑪麗一臉茫然，你問她，這個笑話你有沒有聽懂？這句話英語怎麼說？

👉 你要去上學，你的朋友也正好要開車去，你問他，你可以載我去學校嗎？這句話英語怎麼說？

👉 你正在忙著整理屋子，有朋友來，你問她，你可以幫我一個忙嗎？這句話英語怎麼說？

👉 你去朋友家作客，朋友問你要喝什麼飲料，你想喝咖啡，這句話英語怎麼說？

👉 有人介紹約翰跟你認識，你要跟約翰說，我常常聽別人說起你，這句話英語怎麼說？

👉 公園裡，漂亮的草地旁，常寫著「不要踐踏草地」，這句話英語怎麼說？

這句話英語怎麼說

* 這個笑話你有沒有聽懂？   Did you get the joke?

* 你可以載我去學校嗎？   Can you give me a ride?

* 你可以幫我一個忙嗎？   Can you give me a hand?

* 我要咖啡。   I'll have coffee.

* 我常常聽別人談起你。   I've heard so much about you.

* 請勿踐踏草地。   Keep off the grass.

24

know
[no]

知道的英語就是 know，你如果認識某個人，也可以說你 know 這個人，你也可以 know 一首歌，一個會計軟體。

你叫對方有什麼事通知你，也就是要他讓你 know 這件事。

動詞三態 know, knew, known

精選例句

問問題

* Do you know when the train will arrive?
（你知道火車什麼時候會到嗎？）

* Give him this medicine, and let me know if he's not better in two days.
（給他這個藥，兩天內他如果沒有好轉，通知我。）

* I just know he won't let me do it.
（我知道他不會讓我做。）

* I knew you'd say that.
（我知道你會這麼說。）

* How do you know he'll finish it on time?
（你怎麼知道他會準時做完？）

會某種技能

* Mary knows how to use the accounting software.
（瑪莉知道如何使用這個會計軟體。）

認識

* Do you know the people who live next door?
（你認識住在隔壁的人嗎？）

* Do you know this song?
（你知道這首歌嗎？）

如果你會背一首歌或是一首詞、一首詩、一篇文章那就是你不用看，就記在你的腦子裡、你的心裡了，所以我們說你是 know 那首歌或是那首詞、那首詩、那篇文章 by heart。

◆ I know the song by heart.
（這首歌我會背。）

25

like
[laɪk]

你喜歡任何事物、任何人、任何東西,都可以說 like 那樣東西,那個人,那件事情。

動詞三態 like, liked, liked

問問題

精選例句

* I like Chinese food.
  (我喜歡中國菜。)

* How do you like Taipei?
  (你喜歡台北嗎?)

* Do you like to swim?
  (你喜歡游泳嗎?)

* I didn't like the way he talked to me.
  (我不喜歡他對我說話的方式。)

* John doesn't like anyone talking back to him.
  (約翰不喜歡別人回嘴。)

* I'd like you to be honest with me.
  (我希望你對我誠實。)

隨時說好聽的話，是很受歡迎的一個伎倆，你看到瑪麗穿了一雙新鞋子，你應該趕快過去跟她說 I like your shoes.，瑪麗買了一雙新鞋，有人注意到了，一定很高興，你跟她說這句話，就是含有「你的鞋子很好看」的意思。

◆ I like your shoes.
（我喜歡你的鞋子。）

大家都知道，煮得太熟的牛排不好吃，有人喜歡吃稍微煎一下，還是血淋淋的牛排，但是，有人還是不習慣吃太生的牛排，所以，餐廳都會根據客人的喜好來做牛排，服務生都會問客人要幾分熟的牛排，英語的問法就是，How do you like your steak?（你要幾分熟的牛排？）

◆ How do you like your steak?
（你要幾分熟的牛排？）

◆ How do you like your coffee?
（你的咖啡要不要加糖或奶精？）

26

look
[lʊk]

中文「看」這個字，在英文有 see 和 look 兩個字，see 是人五官的基本功能，也就是「眼睛看得見東西」的意思。look 則是「注意看」的意思，所以，如果你 see 一個美麗的夕陽，忍不住叫你身旁的人看看那美麗的夕陽，就是叫他 look at 那個夕陽。東西掉了，你要找出來，怎麼找呢，那當然要到處 look 了。

一個人看起來很高興，還是很悲傷，就是他 looks happy，或是 looks sad。

動詞三態 look, looked, looked

看

精選例句

* Look at the sunset.
（你看夕陽。）

* Look, there's a deer.
（你看，有一隻鹿。）

* If you look carefully, you'll see what's wrong.
（如果你仔細看，你就會看出錯在哪裡。）

* Sorry, I didn't see. I was looking somewhere else.
（對不起，我沒看到。我剛剛在看別的地方。）

* John looked at his watch and said, "It's late.".
（約翰看他的手錶，說「很晚了」。）

找

* We looked everywhere but we couldn't find it.
（我們到處都找過了，但是找不到。）

* Have you looked under the sofa?
（沙發椅底下你找過了嗎？）

* Did you look in every pocket for the keys?

（找鑰匙，你每一個口袋都找過了嗎？）

* What are you looking for?

（你在找什麼？）

* I'm looking for the remote control.

（我在找遙控器。）

似乎

* Mary looks sad.

（瑪莉好像不太高興。）

* He look tired after the business trip.

（出差回來後，他看起來很累。）

* How do I look in this dress?

（我穿這件洋裝好不好看？）

面向

* Our house looks east, so we get the sun first thing in the morning.

（我們的房子向東，所以早上就有太陽照進來。）

* The hotel looks toward the sea.

（這間旅館面向大海。）

* I like houses that look south.
（我喜歡向南的房子。）

* Our living room looks south.
（我們的客廳向南。）

查看

* I'll have to look at his medical history.
（我必須要看看他的醫療記錄。）

* She wanted the doctor to look at her arms.
（她要醫生檢查她的手臂。）

* The accountant looked closely at his financial records.
（會計師很仔細的看他的財務記錄。）

對事情 的看法

* You'll look at things differently when you're older.
（當你年紀大一點以後，看事情就會有不同。）

look 輕鬆學

☑ It looks like it might rain.

　　看起來好想要下雨。

☑ Look out! There's a car coming.

　　小心，有一部車子來了。

☑ We all look forward to your new book on cooking.

　　我們都在期待你有關烹飪的新書。

☑ You are looking for trouble if you cheat in the exam.

　　如果你考試作弊，那你是在自找麻煩。

⚠ 每天五分鐘

⏱ look like 是個片語，是「好像」的意思。

⏱ look forward to 是個片語，是「期待」的意思。

⏱ Look out! 是叫人家小心，可不是叫人家看外面。

⏱ look for trouble 是「找麻煩」的意思。

大家來說英語

Look, ...

- 在你要跟對方說話之前，先說 look，這只是在用來讓對方知道你有話要說，在你說完 look 這個字之後，接下來要說的，可能是表示「你有話要商量」、「你有不滿意的話要說」、「你要諷刺對方」或是表示「你的態度很堅決」或是「表示安慰」的意思。

☞ Look, can't we talk about it?
（哪，我們不能談一談嗎？）

☞ Look, I've had enough of this.
（嘿，我已經受夠了。）

☞ Look, I didn't mean to.
（嘿，我不是故意的。）

☞ Look, we all make mistakes.
（嘿，誰不會犯錯。）

Look who's here.
（看是誰來了。）

● Look who's here. 是在某個場合遇到熟人，或是有人沒有事先通知，就來拜訪你們時，你表示驚喜的說，「看看是誰來了」。

I'm just looking.
（我只是隨便看看。）

● 當你到商店或百貨公司逛時，若有店員前來問你，May I help you? 時，你就可以回答她說，I'm just looking. 或 I'm only looking. 表示你只是隨便逛逛。

Look who's talking.
（烏鴉不要笑豬黑。）

● 如果你的妹妹常常喜歡把電視機聲音開的很大聲，你屢屢跟她抗議都無效，今天正好你有空，要看個電視輕鬆一下，她正好明天有個很重要的考試，而你卻把電視機聲音開得很大聲，她出來跟你抗議，你就可以回答她說 Look who's talking . 保證她氣得七竅冒煙，卻又拿你沒辦法，因為，你說這句話的意思就是，你自己不是都這麼做嗎？憑什麼說我？

look as if
（看起來）

● 從種種跡象看起來，事情好像是這個樣子囉，例如：
你們等公車等了好久，已經很晚了，你猜測你們可能
錯過最後一班公車了，可能沒有公車會來了，你就說：

☞ There are no buses so it looks as if we'll
be walking home.
（沒有公車了，看起來我們要用走路回家。）

● 一早起來，你看到瑪麗雙眼腫腫的，一副愛睏的樣子，
你就可以這麼跟她說：

☞ You look as if you haven't slept all night.
（你看起來好像整晚沒睡。）

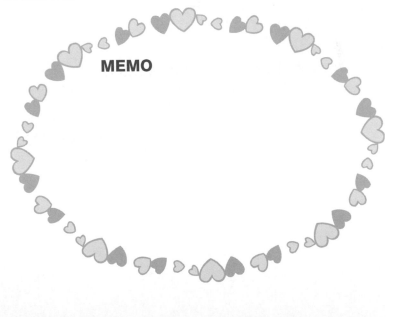

MEMO

27

lose
[luz]

原本屬於你的東西，不再屬於你的了，那你就是 lose 那樣東西，lose 有好事也有壞事，雖然減肥是大家都喜歡的，但是如果你的體重減輕了，你的體重也是算 lose，在股票市場上賠了錢，也是 lose。比賽比輸了，選舉沒選上，都是 lose，

動詞三態　lose, lost, lost

精選例句

失去

* I've lost a lot of weight.
（我體重減輕很多。）

* He can't afford to lose his job. He has a family to support.
（他不能失去他的工作。他要養家。）

* We're going to lose several salesmen.
（我們會失去好幾個售貨員。）

* I lost a lot of money in the stock market.
（我在股票市場輸很多錢。）

* The business is losing money.
（這個生意在賠錢。）

比賽輸了

* When I play tennis with Mary, I always lose.
（我跟瑪莉打網球，我總是輸。）

* Our team lost by ten points.
（我們隊輸十分。）

選舉
沒選上

* John lost the presidential election.
（約翰選總統沒選上。）

丟了

* Make sure you don't lose each other in the crowd.
（要確定你們不要在人群中走失了。）

* Mary lost her son in the crowd.
（在人群中瑪麗的兒子走失了。）

* I've lost my wallet.
（我的皮包丟了。）

你沒有
什麼
損失的

* You have nothing to lose by telling the truth.
（你說實話，沒有什麼損失。）

以下這幾句話，用在你聽不懂，對方跟你解釋的話或教你的話時。

◆ I'm sorry, You've lost me. Could you say it again?
（很抱歉，你把我搞迷糊了。請你再講一遍。）

◆ I'm lost.
（我聽不懂。）

◆ I'm afraid you've lost me there.
（我恐怕你說的話我聽不懂。）

比賽輸了幾分就是 lose by 幾個 points；選舉以幾票之差落選，英語就是 lose by 幾張 votes。

◆ Our team lost by ten points.
（我們隊輸了十分。）

◆ He lost by less than 100 votes.
（他以少於一百票之差落選。）

減肥，就是把重量減輕，英語就是 lose weight。

◆ She is trying to lose weight.
（她正試著在減肥。）

◆ I have lost 10 pounds.
（我已經減了十磅。）

lose 輕鬆學

☐ I'm lost.

我聽不懂。

☐ I lost my temper.

我發脾氣。

☐ We got lost in the big city.

我們在大城市裡迷了路。

☐ Our team lost by ten points.

我們隊輸了十分。

☐ She is trying to lose weight.

她試著在減肥。

每天五分鐘

⏱ I'm lost. 這句話，用在你聽不懂，對方跟你解釋的話或跟你說的話時。

⏱ lose my temper 的 lose 在這裡是「失去控制」的意思，脾氣失去控制就是「發脾氣」的意思。

⏱ lose 在這裡是「迷路」的意思。

⏱ lose by 就是比賽以幾分輸了。

⏱ lose weight 是「減肥」的意思。

28

make
[mek]

製作東西，例如：做生日蛋糕、做衣服、做車子都是 make，如果說某樣東西是在哪裡製作的，英語就是 made in 某個地方，所以在美國買的東西很多都是 made in Taiwan。

動詞三態 make, made, made

製作

* Would you make a cake for Mary's birthday?

（你可不可以做個蛋糕給瑪莉過生日？）

* My mom made the dress for me.

（我的母親做這件洋裝給我。）

* The car was made in Japan.

（這部車子是日本製的。）

* We are making a documentary about World War II.

（我們在製作有關第二次世界大戰的記錄影片。）

* Shall I make you a cup of coffee?

（你要我泡杯咖啡給你嗎？）

使得某人或某樣東西.

* Spoiled milk will make you sick.

（壞了的牛奶會使你生病。）

make 當使役動詞（使；促使；迫使）

- What makes you say that?
  （你為什麼那樣說？）

- We can't make the rock move.
  （我們推不動石頭。）

- Her mother made her do her homework.
  （她的母親強迫她做功課。）

賺錢

* How much do you think she makes?
  （你認為她賺多少錢？）

* I guess she makes about $35,000 a year.
  （我猜她的年薪是三萬五左右。）

* I made $5000 out of selling my car.
  （我賣掉我的車子賺了五千元。）

* She makes good money as a pianist.
  （她當鋼琴家賺很多錢。）

* Our company made a big profit this year.
  （今年我們公司賺很多錢。）

* Mary makes her living by writing books.
（瑪莉靠寫作為生。）

make	
趕上；即時到達	趕到某個特定地方

■ They didn't make the 10 o'clock flight.
（他們沒趕上十點的班機。）

■ Do we have time to make the seven o'clock showing of the movie?
（們有時間趕上七點那一場電影嗎？）

■ Do you think we can make the town before nightfall?
（你認為我們天黑之前可以到鎮上嗎？）

↻ make 在這裡的意思是「能夠去一個已經訂好時間的場合」，它的用法有：make the meeting, make the party, make Friday 等等。

◆ Will you be able to make the Friday meeting?
（星期五的會議你能來參加嗎？）

◆ I'm sorry, I can't make Tuesday after all.
（很抱歉，我星期二終究不能來。）

進學校的校隊，如：球賽的校隊或學科競賽的校隊，英語就是 make **the team**。

♦ John hopes to make the football team this year.
（約翰希望他今年能夠進足球隊。）

♦ Did your sister make the math team?
（你妹妹有沒有進數學校隊？）

make	a decisions（做決定）
	a suggestion（做建議）
	make an appointment（約時間見面）
	made the headlines（成了頭條新聞）

■ He made a quick decision to buy the car.
（他很快的做了決定要買這部車。）

■ May I make a suggestion?
（我可以提個建議嗎？）

■ I'd like to make an appointment with Mr. Lin.
（我要跟林先生約個時間見面。）

■ The scandal made the headlines.
（這件醜聞成了頭條新聞。）

make 輕鬆學

☐ I tried to make friends with Mary, but she didn't seem to like me.

我想跟瑪莉作朋友，但是她好像不喜歡我。

☐ I make my bed every morning.

我每天早上都整理床鋪。

☐ We made believe we were prince and princess.

我們假裝我們是王子和公主。

☐ Can I make up the test I missed?

我可以補考嗎？

☐ What she said was not true. She made it up.

她所說的並不是真的。她杜撰的。

每天五分鐘

⏱ make friends with 就是「跟某人作朋友」的意思。

⏱ make the bed 就是「鋪床、整理床鋪」的意思。

⏱ make believe 是「假裝」的意思。

⏱ make something up 是「補償」或「重做」的意思。

⏱ make something up 也可以是「杜撰」的意思。

make it

● make it 這句口語，基本上的意思是「做得到」的意思，例如：你們快趕不上火車了，所以你說，如果我們用跑的話，應該趕得上，這裡的「趕得上」英語就是 make it，整句話的說法就是，If we run, we should make it.。

● 如果說，某人在某一行業很成功，也可以說某人 make it，例如：有人說她想成為明星，你說，我認為你做不到，英語就是 I don't think you can make it.

● make it 也可以用在「可以參加某個活動或會議」，例如：星期六朋友家有個宴會，你不能去參加，你跟他說抱歉，不能來參加，英語就是 I'm sorry, but I won't be able to make it to the party on Saturday.

make

Make yourself at home.

● Make yourself at home. 這句話是用在，當有人來你家作客時，你要他別拘束，放輕鬆，讓你自己好像在你自己家裡一樣。

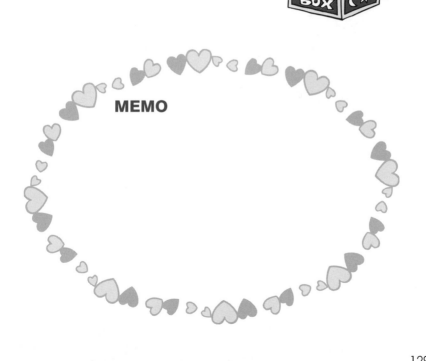

MEMO

29

order
['ɔrdɚ]

order 就是告訴商家你要什麼東西，然後他們就去準備或是進貨，所以，你如果到餐廳去吃飯，要跟服務生 order 你要的菜；你要購買某一本書，書店沒有，你可以跟書店 order，等書來了你再去購買。

order 也可以做「命令」的意思，警察抓到小偷，order 小偷不要動；或是學生不守規矩，老師 order 學生到教室外面去罰站。

動詞三態 order, ordered, ordered

精選例句

點菜

* Will you order for me?
 （請你幫我點菜好嗎？）

* Have you ordered yet?
 （你點菜了嗎？）

* Are you ready to order?
 （你可以點菜了嗎？）

* She ordered the steak meal.
（她點了牛排餐。）

訂購

* I've ordered the book Mary wants to read.
（我已經訂了那本瑪莉想要讀的書。）

* We ordered eggs and bread from the grocery store.
（我們在雜貨店訂購蛋和麵包。）

* I ordered some books from a mail-order company.
（我從一家郵購公司訂購一些書。）

* Shall I order a taxi for you?
（你要我替你叫部計程車嗎？）

命令

* The policeman ordered the thief to put up his hands.
（警察命令小偷把手舉起來。）

* The commandant ordered them to line up against the wall.
（指揮官命令他們靠著牆排好。）

* The teacher ordered John out of the room.
（老師命令約翰到教室外面去。）

30

open
[ˈopən]

open 是「打開」的意思，開門、開香檳、把信打開、開窗戶，都是 open。我們把東西用手打開是 open；商店開門營業或是某家商店新開張也都是 open；花開了，我們也可以說花 open。

動詞三態 open, opened, opened

打開 開始營業

open

開花 新開張

精選例句

打開

* Could you open the door for me?
（你可以替我開門嗎？）

* I'll open a bottle of champagne to celebrate your promotion.
（我開一瓶香檳來慶祝你升遷。）

* She opened the envelope and read the letter.

（她打開信封，看信。）

* She opened the newspaper on the table.

（她翻開桌上的報紙。）

* He opened his arms and welcomed us.

（他張開雙臂歡迎我們。）

開始營業 * What time does your store open?

（你們商店什麼時候開？）

新開張 * They are opening a new supermarket.

（有一家新的超級市場要開張。）

開花 * The roses are starting to open.

（玫瑰開始開花。）

31

pass
[pæs]

你經過某個人的身旁或是某棟建築物、某條街,就是 pass 那個人、某棟建築物、某條街道。你在路上開車,車子開的比其他車子快,超過它,就是 pass 那部車子。

你如果要進入一棟建築,就得 pass through 進那棟建築的門。

河流流經一個城市,也就是 pass through 那個城市;時間流逝,也就好像時間從你身邊 pass 過一樣。

你本來在發燒,現在好了,不再發燒了,也就是說發燒 passed 了。

動詞三態 pass, passed, passed

精選例句

經過

* We passed each other on the staircase.
（我們在樓梯間，錯身而過。）

* Many cars have passed us, but none of them was John's.
（已經有很多部車子過去了，但是沒有一部是約翰的。）

* I think we just passed Main street.
（我想我們剛過了緬因街。）

* We passed the post office on the way home from work yesterday.
（昨天我們下班回家的路上經過郵局。）

超過去、趕過去

* He drove faster in order to pass the car in front of him on the highway.
（他開得快些，以便趕過高速公路上在他前面的那一部車子。）

* He passed the others in the 100-meter race.
（在一百米賽跑中他超過其它的人。）

走過；
穿過

* She passed through the gate.
（她走過大門。）

* When I pass that store, I always look in the windows.
（當我走過那家店的時候，我總是看看櫥窗。）

河流流過

* A beautiful river passes through the city.
（有一條漂亮的河流流經這個城市。）

時間過去

* The days passed by quickly.
（日子很快的過去。）

* Six weeks passed and we still had no news of her.
（六個星期過去了，我們還是沒有她的消息。）

* Several years passed before she got over the loss of her son.
（到她能不再悲痛她兒子的去世，已經是好幾年以後的事了。）

事情過去、
結束

* The fever passed.
（退燒了）

* They waited for the storm to pass .
（他們等著暴風雨結束。）

通過考試、
通過測驗

* My car didn't pass inspection.
（我的車子沒通過檢驗。）

* I passed the English test.
（我英文考及格了。）

* Did John pass the driving test?
（約翰有沒有通過路考？）

通過法律

* The bill was passed by 320 votes to 200.
（這法案以 320 票對 200 票通過。）

傳佈消息

* Please pass along information about the meeting to anyone you see.

（請把開會的消息告訴每個你遇到的人。）

所有權從一個人傳到另一個人

* The house will be passed on to her son when she dies.

（她過世之後，房子會傳給她兒子。）

遞某樣東西給另一個人

* Pass the butter, please.

（請把奶油遞過來。）

* Can you pass me the dictionary?

（把字典遞給我好嗎？）

* Mary passed a note to Jane during class.

（瑪莉在課堂上傳紙條給珍。）

這句話用在你要拿東西給約翰，但是有人正好在你們兩個的中間，所以你就請這個中間人把東西遞給約翰。

◆ Could you pass the card to John, please?

（請你把卡片傳過去給約翰好嗎？）

pass 輕鬆學

☑ John passed the ball to Tom.

約翰把球傳給湯姆。

☑ I passed the driving test.

我通過路考。

☑ When Mary got the news, she passed out.

當瑪莉聽到這個消息的時候,她就昏倒。

☑ His mother passed away last year.

他的母親去年過世。

每天五分鐘

🕐 pass 可以做「傳遞東西給某人」的意思。

🕐 pass 可以做「考試考及格」或是「通過某樣測試」的意思。

🕐 pass out 是「昏倒」的意思。

🕐 pass away 和 pass on 都是「逝世」的意思。

大家來說英語

Pass

- 當有人問你問題，而你不會，你可以說 pass，表示你不會，讓下一個人去回答，或是當你在玩撲克牌時，你這一次不出牌，你也可以說 pass，表示你不出牌，下一位可以繼續。

- 有一道問題，你不會，就可以回答說 I'll have to pass on that one.

Pass me the butter.
（把奶油遞過來）

- 美國人吃的食物跟我們不一樣，他們的正餐不是吃白米飯，而是吃麵包，奶油是是放在桌上，用餐時每個人自己抹奶油在麵包上，下次你看電影時，注意看美國人用餐時，常常在餐桌上叫著別人 Pass the butter, please.

- 美國人在做菜時，通常也盡量不要加調味料，這是尊重個人的喜好，要加多少鹽、要加多少胡椒，用餐時自己加，所以，在餐桌上你也常常可以聽到有人叫別人 Pass the salt,please.（請把鹽罐子遞過來。）

這句話英語怎麼說

- 👉 大家要一起唱一首歌,有人拿出歌詞來要給你看,你說,這首歌我會背,這句話英語怎麼說?

- 👉 在海邊,你看到夕陽好美,你叫大家看那夕陽,這句話英語怎麼說?

- 👉 你到百貨公司去逛街,有店員過來問你要買什麼嗎,你要回答他說,我只是隨便看看,這句話英語怎麼說?

- 👉 你知道約翰要去參加學校數學校隊的甄選,事後你問他,你有沒有進數學校隊?這句話英語怎麼說?

- 👉 你到餐廳去吃飯,服務生過來問你可以點菜了嗎,這句話英語怎麼說?

這句話英語怎麼說

* 這首歌我會背。   I know the song by heart.

* 看那夕陽。   Look at the sunset.

* 我只是隨便看看。   I'm just looking.

* 我完全聽不懂。   I'm lost.

* 你有沒有進數學校隊?   Did you make the math team?

* 你可以點菜了嗎?   Are you ready to order?

32

pay
[pe]

天下沒有白吃的午餐，不管你是吃飯、買東西、電話費、房租，甚至於受教育，樣樣你都得 pay。即使公司老闆請你工作，他也 pay 你薪水。

動詞三態 pay, paid, paid

付錢　pay　付工資、薪水

精選例句

付錢

* Let's each pay our own way.
（我們各付各的。）

* He paid his own way through college.
（他自己賺錢完成大學學業。）

* May I pay by credit card?
（我可以用信用卡付帳嗎？）

* I'll pay cash.
  （我要付現金。）

* John paid some kids to wash the car.
  （他付錢給一些小孩子幫他洗車。）

* I paid her $50 for the book.
  （我以五十元跟她買了這本書。）

* Have you paid the phone bill yet?
  （你電話費繳了沒有？）

付工資、
薪水
* How much do they pay you?
  （他們付你多少錢？）

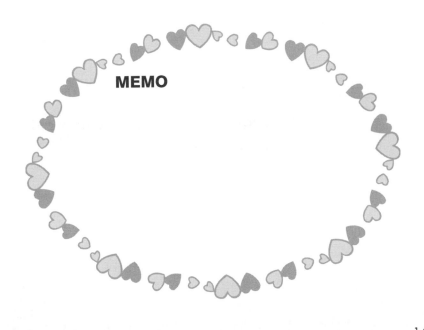

MEMO

33

play
[ple]

play 這個字是「遊玩」的意思，要捉弄別人就是對那個人 play 一個 trick（把戲），玩某樣東西就是 play with 那樣東西，例如：play with matches（玩火柴），打球也就是在 play 那個球類：例如 play basketball，彈奏任何樂器的英語就是 play 那樣樂器。在一場戲劇中扮演某個角色，也就是 play 那個角色。如果有人在裝傻，他就是在 play dumb。

動詞三態 play, played, played

精選例句

遊玩

* She watched the children play in the playground.
（她看著小孩子在遊樂場玩耍。）

* Mary played a trick on John.
（瑪莉捉弄約翰。）

* The children are playing with a ball in the back yard.
（小朋友在後院玩球。）

* Don't play with matches.
（不要玩火柴。）

play （打球，玩牌）	football（打足球）
	chess（玩西洋棋）
	cards（打撲克牌）

■ Do you like to play golf?
（你喜歡打高爾夫球嗎？）

■ We won't be ready to play against the other team this weekend.
（這個週末我們還不能跟另一隊打。））

■ The Giants are playing the Cowboys tomorrow.
（巨人隊明天要跟牛仔隊比賽。）

播放音樂、
彈奏樂器

* Mary is playing the piano.
（瑪麗在彈鋼琴。）

* I've always wanted to learn to play the violin.
（我一直想學拉小提琴。）

* I could hear a flute playing Christmas songs next door.
（我可以聽到隔壁，長笛吹著聖誕歌曲。）

play（表演）	
演戲時飾演某一個角色	某一個戲劇在上演

■ I'd like to play Snow White.
（我要飾演白雪公主。）

■ "Cats" is playing at the Majesty Theater now.
（『貓』這齣音樂劇現在在皇家戲院上演。）

假裝　　　* Don't play dumb in the principal's office.
（在校長辦公室裡別裝傻。）

起作用；　* He played a huge part in yesterday's
有影響　　football game.
（他對昨天的足球賽有很大的影響。）

出牌　　　* She couldn't decide which card to play.
（她沒辦法決定要出哪一張牌。）

MEMO

34

put
[pʊt]

把東西放在某個地方，就是 put 這樣東西在某個地方，把人安排在某個時段工作，例如：讓他做小夜班，也就是 put 他在小夜班。

一個人最看重什麼事情。就會把這件事放在第一位，有人 put 家庭優先，有人 put 事業優先，有人 put 金錢優先。

把字寫下，也就是 put 這些字在紙上，做一件事你放多少時間進去，就是 put 多少時間進去。

動詞三態 put, put, put

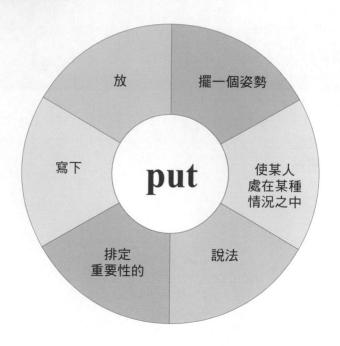

精選例句

放

* Put those books on the shelf.
（把那些書放在架子上。）

* Where did you put the keys?
（你把鑰匙放在哪裡？）

* You put too much salt in the soup.
（你在湯裡放太多鹽。）

* They put him on the second shift.
（他們把他排在小夜班。）

擺一個
姿勢

* Put your hand up if you have questions.
（如果你有問題就把手舉起來。）

使某人處
在某種情
況之中

* The news has put us in a bad mood.
（這個消息使我們的心情都很壞。）

* The sound of the waves put me to sleep.
（海浪的聲音催我入睡。）

* The doctor put him in the emergency room.
（醫生把他放在急診室裡。）

說法

     * Put your question clearly.
      （把你的問題說清楚。）

     * Can you put your problem in simple words?
      （你可以用簡單的話，說你的問題嗎？）

排定重要性的

     * He puts his family first.
      （他把他的家庭放在第一位。）

寫下

     * Put your name at the top of each answer sheet.
      （把你的名字寫在每張答案紙的上端。）

放時間進去

     * I hope you like it. I've put so much time into it.
      （我希望你喜歡。我已經花了很多時間去做。）

put 輕鬆學

☐ Did you put sugar in my coffee?

我的咖啡你有沒有加糖？

☐ She put up her hand to ask a question.

她舉手要問一個問題。

☐ It's cold outside. You'd better put on your coat.

外面很冷。你最好穿上大衣。

☐ The meeting has been put off until tomorrow.

會議延期到明天。

☐ Stop putting me on.

別騙我。

每天五分鐘

🕐 把糖放入咖啡裡，或是把鹽放入湯裡，英語都是 put。

🕐 put up 某人的 hand，就是把手舉起來。put 在這句話裡是過去式，不加 s。

🕐 put on 是「穿上衣服」的意思。

🕐 put off 是「延期」的意思。

🕐 put 某人 on 的意思就是「開他的玩笑」，或是「騙他」。

run 最基本的意思就是「跑」,你平常跑步,或是為了趕公車趕快跑,都是在 run。

run 一個店,就是在經營那個店。

人在跑是 run,車子可以開,跑得很好或是某件機器,某個系統運作的順利,也是在 run。

如果你要競選一個職位,你就是要 run for 那個職位,如果你要跟約翰競選一個職位,你就是要 run against 約翰 for 那個職位。

run

[rʌn]

動詞三態 run, ran, run

跑

* If we run, we should catch the bus.
  （如果我們用跑的話，我們應該可以趕上公車。）

* Are you going to run the marathon?
  （你要參加馬拉松比賽嗎？）

* John is running in the 100-meter race.
  （約翰在跑一百公尺賽跑。）

* Run and tell Mary "X Files" is on.
  （你趕快去告訴瑪莉『X 檔案』在演了。）

要離開某個地方

* It's late. I've got to run now.
  （已經很晚了。我該走了。）

經營

* I would like to run my own cafe one day.
  （有一天我想自己開一間小館子。）

* Could you run the store for me while I'm gone?
  （我不在的時候，你可以幫我看店嗎？）

競選

* I am going to run against John for PTA president.
  （我要跟約翰競選家長會會長。）

* Did you hear who is running against Bush?

（你有沒有聽說誰要跟布希競選？）

* Do you know who is running for president?

（你知道誰要競選總統嗎？）

* Who is planning to run for mayor?

（誰計畫要競選市長？）

操作、機器的運轉

* Is your new car running okay?

（你的車子跑得還好嗎？）

* The new system won't be up and running until next month.

（新系統要在下個月才能裝好，開始運轉。）

* Do you know how to run a tractor?

（你知道如何操作拖拉機嗎？）

車子在跑動

* The buses don't run on Sundays.

（公車星期天不開。）

* The bus runs past my house every hour.

（公車每一個小時經過我家一次。）

| 水或液體
的流動 | * Don't leave the faucet running.
（別讓水龍頭流個不停。） |

* Run a bath
（把浴缸放滿水。）

* Could you run me a hot bath?
（請你幫我準備好一缸熱的洗澡水，好嗎？）

ran an ad（登廣告）
run a temperature（發燒）
run late（超過預定的時間）
run first（跑第一名）

■ We ran an ad to hire an editor.
（我們登廣告要請一位編輯。）

■ Mary is running a temperature of a 40-degree.
（瑪莉發燒到四十度。）

■ The meeting is running late. It won't be over until 11:00.
（會議超過預定的時間，不到十一點是不會結束的。）

■ He ran first in the 100-meter race.
（他在一百米賽跑中得第一名。）

🔄 如果你洗衣服時，其中一件紅色的衣服染到其他的衣服，那英語就是 the color ran.

◆ **The color ran when my mom washed my red shirt.**
（當我母親洗我的紅色襯衫時，顏色染到其他的衣服。）

🔄 如果紙張弄濕了，紙上的墨水也會糊掉，它的英語就是， the ink on the letter ran。

◆ **Look, the ink on the letter ran.**
（你看，這封信上的墨水糊掉了。）

🔄 襪子、褲襪 run，就是「襪子、褲襪破了」。

◆ **Her pantyhose ran and made a big hole.**
（她的褲襪破了一個大洞。）

run 輕鬆學

☑ Can you run fast?

你可以跑得很快嗎？

☑ I often go running before work.

我上班之前常出去跑跑步。

☑ I've got to run an errand. I'll be back in a minute.

我有事情要去做。一會兒就回來。

☑ We are running low on eggs.

我們的蛋剩下不多。

☑ I ran out of milk while I was baking the cakes.

我在做蛋糕的時候，牛奶都用完了。

每天五分鐘

🕐 run 就是「跑步」的意思。

🕐 go running 就是「去跑跑步」當作一種運動。

🕐 run an errand 就是「做一些雜物」的意思。

🕐 run low on 某樣東西，就是「某樣東西不夠」或「某樣東西剩下不多」的意思。

🕐 run out of 某樣東西，就是「把某樣東西通通用完」的意思。

It runs in the family.
（這是家傳的。）

● 當我們說到某人很聰明，事實上他家裡每一個人都很聰明，英語的說法就是 It runs in the family. 意思是說「他的聰明是家傳的」。又如：某人的頭髮是紅色的，而你知道她家每個人的頭髮都是紅色的，英語的說法也是這句話 It runs in the family.

Run and get your coat.
（去拿你的外套）

● 天冷了，你家小孩要出門，你叫他去房間裡拿件外套穿，你就可以跟他說 Run and get your coat.（去拿你的外套）

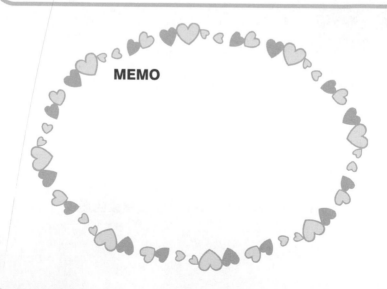

MEMO

 這句話英語怎麼說

- 你要出門，卻找不到鑰匙，你問先生，你把鑰匙放在哪裡？這句話英語怎麼說？

- 你在朋友家作客，天晚了，你說，我該走了，這句話英語怎麼說？

- 你要做蛋糕，打開冰箱，發現冰箱裡的蛋剩下不多，你說，我們的蛋快沒有了，這句話英語怎麼說？

- 你的朋友買了新車，你問他，你的新車好開嗎？這句話英語怎麼說？

這句話英語怎麼說

* 你把鑰匙放在哪裡？　　Where did you put the keys?

* 我該走了。　　　　　　I've got to run.

* 我們的蛋快沒有了。　　We are running low on eggs.

* 你的新車好開嗎？　　　Is your new car running okay?

36

say
[se]

開口把你要讓別人知道的話說出來，就是 say。
你想知道現在是幾點，你看手錶或是時鐘，它會讓
你知道現在是幾點的，雖然手錶或時鐘不會說話，
但是手錶或是時鐘上面寫的時間就好像在 say（跟
你說）現在是幾點。

動詞三態 say,said,said

精選例句

說話

* What did Mary say?
  （瑪莉說什麼？）

* Mary said she would do the dishes.
  （瑪莉說她會洗碗。）

* She didn't say when she will be back.
  （她沒有說她什麼時候會回來。）

* I don't believe anything he says.
  （我不相信他所說的。）

* Does anyone else have anything to say?
（有誰還要說什麼嗎？）

say a few words
簡短的說明一下

■ I'd just like to say a few words about the plan.
（關於這個計畫，我只想要簡短的說明一下。）

■ Remember to say good-bye when you're leaving.
（你要離開的時候，要說再見。）

■ Did you say thanks to the driver when you got off the bus?
（你下車的時候有沒有跟司機說謝謝？）

法律規定 * The law says anyone under 18 can't buy cigarettes.
（法律規定任何人十八歲以下不可以買香菸。）

用寫的消息或數字 * My watch says it's 5:30.
（我手錶的時間是五點三十分。）

* What did Mary say in her letter?
（瑪莉的信上說什麼？）

161

* It said in the paper that 200 people were killed.

（報上說有兩百個人被殺。）

意思是

* What do you think the writer is saying in this book?

（你認為作者這本書要說什麼？）

* Are you saying I'm not qualified?

（你的意思是說我不夠資格？）

* So what you are saying is, you don't want to join us.

（那你的意思是說，你不想加入我們。）

建議、 假設

* I say we should give him a piece of our mind.

（我建議我們應該好好的說他一頓。）

↻ 以上兩句話裡，**say** 的意思就是「假設某件事會發生」的意思。

◆ Let's say you fail the test, then what?

（假設你考不及格，那又怎麼樣？）

◆ Just say you won the lottery. What would you do?

（假設你贏得彩券。你要做什麼？）

●●●● 大家來說英語 ●●●●

say yes

● 如果你要朋友跟你一起去看電影，她還猶疑不決，可能有拒絕的意思，你要求她答應，英語可以說，Oh, please say yes!（噢，拜託你說一聲『好』。）

say so

● 如果有人問你一件事，例如：對方問你，你認為會下雨嗎，而你認為不會，英語的說法就是，I wouldn't say so.

37

see
[si]

see 這個字最基本上就是「眼睛看見東西」的意思，如果，你是電影院的守門人，有人要進入電影院，那你就得 see 他有沒有門票，這裡的 see 除了用眼睛看之外，還有檢查一下的意思。做人要會察言觀色，有人在生氣，你要 see（看得出來），有些事情不是用眼睛去看，而是用心靈去 see，也就是用心靈去瞭解，或是用腦子去判斷、想像。

動詞三態 see, saw, seen

精選例句

看

* I can't see a thing without my glasses.
（我不戴眼鏡看不到東西。）

* Did you see the sign?
（你有沒有看到牌子？）

* I saw a turtle as I was going to work this morning.
（今早我要去上班的時候，看到一隻烏龜。）

察看

* Can I see your ticket?
（請把票拿給我看。）

* Go and see if the oven is off.
（去看看火爐有沒有關。）

瞭解

* I can see that you're angry.
（我看得出你在生氣。）

* Mary looks very tired. I can see why.
（瑪莉看起來很累。我知道為什麼。）

* Do you see what I mean?
（你知道我的意思嗎？）

* Do you see the point of the joke?
（你聽得懂這個笑話在說什麼嗎？）

想像

* I can't see him objecting to it.
（我不認為他會反對這件事。）

確定
* See that the door is locked
（要確定門有上鎖。）

經歷
* Our town has seen many changes.
（我們鎮上已經改變很多。）

你要 see 某人，除非她是個大美人，否則你的目的絕不是單純的去看她，而是另有目的去拜訪；另外，我們如果說 John is seeing Mary，除非是約翰正目不轉晴的在看著瑪麗，否則這句話的意思是指約翰和瑪麗在交往中。至於你生病了，要去看醫生，英語就是 see a doctor。

見面、拜訪

* I want to see Mr. Lin.
（我要見林先生。）

* When you are in the town, come to see us.
（你到本市來的時候，過來看我們。）

* We're going to see Mary. Do you want to come along?
（我們要去看瑪莉，你要不要一起來？）

無意中遇見

* I saw Mary at the post office this morning.
（今天早上我在郵局遇到瑪莉。）

會客

* She doesn't want to see anyone at the moment.
（她此刻不想見任何人。）

與別人幽會

* I heard John is seeing another woman.
（我聽說約翰在跟另一個女人交往。）

看醫生

* You should go see a doctor.
（你應該去看醫生。）

see	
再見	送行

再見

* See you later.
（再見。）

* I'll be seeing you.
（再見。）

* See you around.
（再見。）

送行

* I'll see you to the door.
（我送你到門口。）

* Do you need me to see you back to the dorm?
（你要我送你回宿舍嗎？）

* I'll be back as soon as I see Mary home.
（我送瑪莉回家之後，會馬上回來。）

see 輕鬆學

☑ We went to the airport to see Mary off.
我們到機場給瑪莉送行。

☑ They are happy to see the last of John.
他們很高興以後不會再看到約翰。

☑ I hear the doorbell. Will someone see to the door?
我聽到門鈴聲,有沒有人要去應門?

☑ See you! 再見。

☑ See you later. 再見。

☑ See you around. 有空再見。

每天五分鐘

🕐 see 某人 off,就是「去給某人送行」。

🕐 see the last of 某人,就是「最後一次看到他,以後不會再看到他了」。

🕐 see to 某件事,就是「照料一下這件事」。

🕐 See you! 是用在跟別人道別,而你知道你還會再見到對方時。

🕐 See you later. 是跟對方說「待會兒見」,也就是你跟對方道別,但是你很快就會再見到他。

🕐 See you around. 是跟對方道別,但是沒有約什麼時候會再見面。

38

send
[sɛnd]

把東西寄送給某人的英語是 send，這個字不僅可以 send 東西，也可以 send 人，那就是把這個人派出去做事情，或是送他去某個地方的意思。

把東西或人送到某個地方去是 send，讓某人進入某種狀態中，英語就是說 send 他 into 某種狀態。

動詞三態 send, sent, sent

精選例句

寄送、派遣、送某人到某個地方

* I'd like to send the letter by airmail.
（我要用航空寄這封信。）

* I'll send Mary a card to congratulate her.
（我要寄一張卡片給瑪莉，跟她恭喜。）

* She sent John to buy some milk.
（她派約翰去買牛奶。）

* They sent their son to America to study.
（他們把他們的兒子送到美國讀書。）

對某人產生某種影響

* His rude remark sent her into a rage.
（他無禮的話讓她很生氣。）

* His boring speech sent me into sleep.
（他乏味的演講，催我入睡。）

你住旅館時，要叫客房服務派人送東西來你的房間給你，你就要叫客房服務 send up 你要的東西。

◆ Could you send up two glasses of orange juice?
（請你派人送兩杯柳橙汁上來。）

有人病了，你就該 send for（派人去請）醫生來。

◆ Mary is ill. Please send for a doctor.
（瑪莉病了，請派人請醫生來。）

39

sell
[sɛl]

把東西給別人以換來金錢，英語就是 sell。

東西有人購買，就是這樣東西可以 sell，東西賣的好就是這樣東西 sell well。

動詞三態 sell, sold, sold

賣

sell

有人購買

賣

精選例句

* I'll sell you my car for $2000.
  （我把車賣你兩千元。）

* If I offer you another hundred, will you sell?
  （如果我多出一百元，你要賣嗎？）

* John is selling his car for $1000.
  （約翰的車子要賣一千元。）

有人購買   * His new book sold well.
（他的新書賣得很好。）

* Their last album sold millions.
（他們上一張唱片賣了幾百萬。）

sell out
賣光

■ All the tickets are sold out.
（所有的票都賣光了。）

> 問商店他們有沒有賣某樣東西，要問 **Do you sell** 某樣東西？
>
> ◆ Do you sell boots?
> （你們有賣馬靴嗎？）

40

speak
[spik]

跟某人交談的英語就是 speak，你打電話給瑪麗，你肯定是要跟瑪麗說話，你可以跟接電話的人說 May I speak with Mary? 或 May I speak to Mary? 可是，你如果要找人談事情，通常你會跟他說，我要 speak with you。

speak 也可以做「發出聲音說話」的意思，所以如果你喉嚨痛，你可就沒辦法 speak 了。人類會說話，說的話可不是只有聲音，而是可以彼此溝通的話叫做語言，所以會說某種語言，也就是會 speak 那種語言。你也可以在一個正式場合，在台上對台下所有的來賓 speak（正式發表演說）。

動詞三態 speak, spoke, spoken

精選例句

跟某人談話、談事情

* John would like to speak with you for a moment.

（約翰要跟你談一下。）

跟某人說話

* I'm angry with him and I refuse to speak to him.

（我生他的氣，我拒絕跟他說話。）

* They had a fight and are not speaking to each other.

（他們吵架了，彼此不講話。）

發出聲音說話

* I was so shocked I couldn't speak.

（我嚇得講不出話來。）

* He can't speak because of a sour throat.

（他喉嚨痛不能說話。）

會講某一種語言

* Do you speak English?

（你會說英語嗎？）

正式發表演說	* Who is going to speak at the conference? （這次會議誰要來演說？）
	* The President will speak on television tonight. （總統將在今晚的電視上演說。）
談論某件事情	* The policeman spoke of the accident. （警察談論這次的車禍。）

speak up
講大聲一點

■ I can hardly hear you.
（我幾乎聽不到你說的話。）

■ Would you speak up?
（你講大聲一點好嗎？）

> 告訴接電話的人，或是接待的人，你要找某人談話。

◆ May I speak with Mary?
（我想跟瑪莉談話。）

 這句話英語怎麼說

- 瑪麗跟你們說話，你卻沒有聽清楚，你問約翰，瑪麗說什麼？ 這句話英語怎麼說？

- 約翰已經有女朋友，卻又跟珍妮在約會，你說，約翰跟另一個 女人在幽會，這句話英語怎麼說？

- 瑪麗病了，你要跟她說，你應該去看醫生，這句話英語怎麼 說？

- 約翰出版了一本新書，賣得很好，你說，他的新書賣得很好， 這句話英語怎麼說？

- 你打電話到瑪麗家，想跟瑪麗講電話，你跟接電話的人說，你 想跟瑪麗講話，這句話英語怎麼說？

這句話英語怎麼說

* 瑪麗說什麼？	What did Mary say?
* 約翰跟另一個女人在幽會。	John is seeing another woman.
* 你應該去看醫生。	You should go see a doctor.
* 他的新書賣的很好。	His new book sold well.
* 我想跟瑪麗講話。	May I speak with Mary?

41

start
[start]

開始做任何事情都是 start，你開始上電腦課 start the computer lessons，或是開始看一本書 start a book。開始做一件事，可以說 start doing 或是 start to do，例如：start getting dressed（開始穿衣服），也可以說 start to get dressed。

動詞三態 start, started, started

精選例句

開始

* Let's start the computer lessons in June.
（我們六月開始上電腦課吧。）

* You'd better start getting dressed soon.
（你最好趕快開始穿衣服。）

* I've just started learning English.
（我剛開始學英語。）

* She started to laugh.
（她開始笑。）

* It started to rain.
（天開始下雨。）

* Spring break starts on April 2.
（春假四月二號開始。）

請求幫忙　* The show starts at 7:30.
（表演七點三十分開始。）

* I only started this book yesterday.
（我昨天才開始看這本書。）

* You'll have to start early to get to Chicago before nightfall.
（你們得早點開始，才能在天黑之前到芝加哥。）

start	開始上學
	開始上班
	開始一項事業
	一天之始
	車子發動

開始上學　* My son is starting school in September.
（我兒子九月要開始上學。）

開始上班　* I got a job and will start next week.
（我找到工作，下星期開始上班。）

開始
一項事業

＊ He quit his job and started his own business last year.
（他去年辭掉工作，開始他自己的事業。）

＊ John started his own publishing business last year.
（約翰去年開始他自己的出版事業。）

一天之始

＊ John always starts the day with a cup of coffee.
（約翰早上總是要喝一杯咖啡。）

開始
一項事業

＊ The car just won't start.
（車子就是發不動。）

＊ I couldn't get my car started this morning.
（今天早上，我的車子不能發動。）

MEMO

42

stay
[ste]

在某一個地方停留，就是 stay 在那兒，你要朋友留下來吃飯，就是請他 stay for dinner。stay 這個字加以引伸，也可以是說「保持在某一狀況不變」，例如：天氣一整天都 stayed bad（都是保持在不好的狀況），在宴會中大家都喝醉了，只有你一個人 stay sober（保持在清醒的狀態）。

動詞三態 stay, stayed, stayed

停留、逗留

居留、暫住

保持某一狀況

stay

精選例句

停留、逗留

* Can you stay for dinner?
（你可以留下來吃晚飯嗎？）

* I can't stay long. I'll have to leave soon.
（我不能留太久。我很快就要走。）

* She stayed at the office and worked late.
（她留在辦公室裡，工作到很晚。）

居留、暫住

* My parents are staying with us for a few days.
（我的父母要在我家住幾天。）

* She was staying in the same hotel as I.
  （她跟我住同一個旅館。）

* How long will you stay here?
  （你要在這裡住多久？）

保持某一狀況

* The weather stayed bad all day.
  （一整天天氣都很不好。）

* The unemployment rate stayed below three percent.
  （失業率保持在 3% 以下。）

* I'm the only one who stayed sober at the party.
  （我是宴會中唯一保持清醒的人。）

* Stay away from my computer.
  （別碰我的電腦。）

stay up	熬夜

■ If I stay up, I'm sleepy the next day.
（如果我熬夜，隔天我會想睡覺。）

■ I can't stay up that late.
（我不能熬到那麼晚。）

stay over	在別人家過夜

■ Can I stay over at Mary's tonight?
（我可以在瑪莉家過夜嗎？）

43

talk
[tɔk]

talk 是「跟別人說話」或是「開口說話」的意思，你跟約翰談話，可以說 talk with John，或 talk to John，但是要談論一件事情，則是 talk about 那件事情。如果你犯了罪，法官要你 talk，他可不是要你隨便說一說話，他可是要你「招供」。

動詞三態 talk, talked, talked

精選例句

跟某人說話

* Who was that you were talking to at the party?

（宴會中跟你說話的是誰？）

* Lovers talk with their eyes.

（戀人用眉目傳情。）

跟某人某件嚴肅的事情

* I need to talk with you about my salary.

（我要跟你談談我的薪水問題。）

開口說話

* Most babies start to talk by 18 months.

（大多數的嬰孩十八個月時開始說話。）

* Can you imagine that computers would be able to talk?

（電腦會說話，你能想像得到嗎？）

招供

* Though they tortured him, he refused to talk.

（雖然他們拷問他，但是他拒絕招供。）

talk about	談論

■ We were talking about the blackout last night.
（我們正在談昨晚停電的事。）

> 如果兩個人 are not talking，表示「他們兩個人吵架，彼此都拒絕跟對方說話」。
>
> ◆ Mary and John are not talking.
> （瑪莉和約翰兩個人彼此不講話。）

talk	sports（談論體育）
	politics（談論政治）
	business（談生意）

■ Stop talking sports. Let's talk business.
（不要談體育。我們來談生意吧。）

44

take
[tek]

你要到圖書館去，你看天色陰沈，可能會下雨，所以你就決定 take an umbrella with you，也就是你要去圖書館，你帶著雨傘到圖書館去。你的妹妹瑪麗想看電影，媽媽要你 take Mary to a movie，也就是媽媽要你帶瑪麗去看電影。

動詞三態 take,took,taken

take	某人	with you	到你要去的地方
	某物		

不管你要去什麼地方，把這樣東西帶著去。帶著某人跟你去你要去的地方。我會帶某人去我要去的地方。

- ◆ Take an umbrella with you. It looks like it will rain.

  （帶把傘，看起來會下雨。）

- ◆ When you go to the movies, can you take Mary with you?

  （如果你要去看電影，可不可以帶瑪莉一起去？）

- ◆ I'll take Mary with me when I go to the party.

  （我要去參加宴會時，會帶瑪莉一起去。）

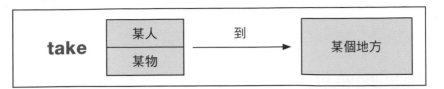

帶瑪麗去看電影，帶瑪麗去參加宴會。帶我去商店，帶我去逛街。把車子拿去修車廠，把東西拿到我的房間。

◆ Why don't you take Mary to a movie?
（為什麼不帶瑪莉去看電影？）

◆ I'll take Mary with me when I go to the fair.
（我要去市集的時候，會帶瑪莉一起去。）

◆ Can you take me to the store?
（你可以帶我去商店嗎？）

◆ John took our car to the garage to be repaired.
（約翰把我們的車子開去修車廠修理。）

◆ May I take your bags to your room?
（你要我把你的行李拿到你的房間嗎？）

take	a vacation（度假）
	a walk（散步）
	a bath（洗澡）
	a shower（洗淋浴）
	a 10-day trip（十天的旅行）

187

- We take a vacation every May.
  （我們每年五月都去度假。）

- I'm going to take a walk. Do you want to come along?
  （我要去散步。你要不要一起來？）

- It's time for you to take a bath.
  （你該去洗澡了。）

- Do you take shower every the morning?
  （你每天早上都淋浴嗎？）

- We would like to take a 10-day trip.
  （我們要去旅行十天。）

精選例句

需要

* It took us two hours to get there.
  （我們花了兩小時才能到那裡。）

* How long will it take to type the letter?
  （打這封信要多久？）

* How many stamps will this letter take?
  （這封信需要幾張郵票？）

* How long does first class mail take?
  （第一類郵件要多久才會到？）

修課

* I am planning to take English with Ms. Lin.
  （我計畫上林老師的英文課。）

* I am taking two science classes this semester.
  （這學期我上了兩門科學課。）

* I only had to take 6 credit hours my senior year.
  （我大四只需修六學分的課。）

吃

* He took some tea with his lunch.
  （他吃午餐時也喝茶。）

* Do you want to take lunch together?
  （你要不要一起去吃午餐？）

接受

 * If I were you, I'd take the job.
  （如果我是你，我會接受這個工作。）

 * Do you take credit cards?
  （你們收信用卡嗎？）

 * Do you take traveler's checks?
  （你們收旅行支票嗎？）

 * The car only takes unleaded.
  （這部車子只能加無鉛汽油。）

吃藥

 * Do you want to take an aspirin for your headache?
  （你頭痛要不要吃一顆阿斯匹靈？）

 * John was caught taking drugs.
  （約翰被抓到吃毒品。）

**有空位
容納**

 * The car won't take any more people.
  （這部車沒辦法再容納任何一個人。）

承受

 * How did she take it when she got fired?
  （她被開除的時候，還能承受嗎？）

↻ 這句話是用在購物或商務談判，你決定要買或接受條件時的說法。

◆ I'll take it.
 （好，我要了。

take 輕鬆學

☐ Do you take sugar in your coffee?
你的咖啡要加糖嗎？

☐ Did you take notes in the class?
你課堂上有記筆記嗎？

☐ He always takes sides with Mary.
他總是偏袒瑪莉。

☐ Don't let her innocent smile take you in.
別讓她天真無邪的笑容把你騙了。

☐ Will you take care of my plants while I'm away?
我不在的時候，你可以照料我的花草嗎？

每天五分鐘

🕐 take notes 上課的時候記筆記。

🕐 take sides 就是「偏袒」的意思，偏袒某人或偏袒某一邊，英語就是 take sides with 某人或某一邊。

🕐 take 某人 in，就是「欺騙某人」的意思。

🕐 take care of 就是「照顧、照料」的意思。

Don't take me wrong.
（別誤會我的意思。）

● 大家在討論「非常光碟」的事件，你說你不認同非常
  光碟的作法，一看其他的人都氣勢洶洶的瞪著你，趕
  快見風轉舵說 Don't take me wrong.（各位別誤會我的
  意思），我是贊同言論自由的。

Could I take a message?
（你要留話嗎？）

● 有人打電話來要找你哥哥聽電話，但是你哥哥不在
  家，你會告訴打電話的人，你哥哥不在家，說完這句
  話，你通常還可以問他 Could I take a message?，你
  問這句話是在問他要不要留話給你哥哥，讓你代轉，
  至於要不要留話，就要由對方決定了。

Take it easy.
（別太激動。）

● 你的朋友不知為了什麼事，氣沖沖的，你一看，趕緊
  跟他說，Take it easy.（別太激動），到底發生了什麼
  事，你慢慢講，沒有什麼大不了的事，別氣壞了身
  體。

Take care.
（保重。）

● Take care. 這句話常用在兩個人互道再見的時候，你跟他說 Good bye. 之後，加一句 Take care. 可真窩心啊。

MEMO

45

tell
[tɛl]

你 talk with 約翰，或是 speak with 約翰，那是跟約翰說話，如果你 tell 約翰，則是你告訴他一件事情，或是告訴他該怎做，不是跟他說話。講故事的英語就是 tell a story. 如果有人在生氣，你看得出來他在生氣，那就是你可以 tell 他在生氣，tell 可以做「看得出來、會分辨」的意思。如果約翰考試作弊，你就可以警告他說，我要去 tell your mother on you，這裡的 tell on 某人就是去揭發別人所做的壞事。

動詞三態 tell, told, told

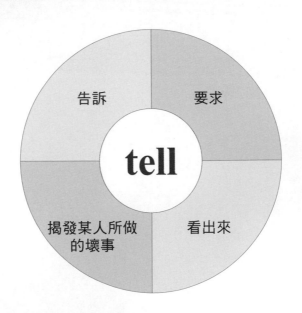

告訴

* Could you tell me a bedtime story?
  （你能不能跟我講一個床邊故事？）

* Tell us about your vacation.
  （跟我們講你去度假的情形。）

* I told you she wouldn't help you.
  （我告訴你了，她不會幫你忙。）

* The beeper tells you that you've left the lights on.
  （嗶嗶聲在告訴你，你沒關燈。）

要求

* Stop trying to tell me what to do all the time.
  （不要總是告訴我要怎麼做。）

* Don't tell me how to behave in public.
  （不要告訴我在公眾場合要怎麼做。）

* The teacher told all the children to stop talking.
  （老師要所有的小朋友不要再說話。）

看出來

＊ How can you tell he dyed his hair?

（你怎麼看得出來他的頭髮染了顏色？）

＊ I could tell she was mad at me.

（我看得出來她生我的氣。）

＊ I could tell it was John by the way he walks.

（從他走路的樣子，我就看得出來那是約翰。）

＊ I can never tell Jack and John apart.

（我沒辦法分得出，誰是傑克、誰是約翰。）

＊ I have trouble telling the difference between a gerund and a participle.

（動名詞和分詞的區別，我分不出來。）

揭發某人所做的壞事

＊ I'm going to tell your mother on you.

（我要去跟你母親說你所做的壞事。）

●●●● 大家來說英語 ●●●●

You're telling me.
（就是說嘛！）

● You're telling me. 這句話用在，當有人說一件事，這件事你已經知道，而且你也同意他的說法時，例如：天氣很熱，約翰走進來，說「這種天氣真令人受不了」，而你也正覺得熱得受不了，你就可以回答說 You're telling me.

Tell me about it!
（我知道。）

● 今天是期末考的最後一天，一連考了五天，都快把你給烤焦了，終於考完了，回到宿舍，正疲累不堪，癱在沙發椅上喘氣，你的室友進來，也是往床上一躺，說累死我了，簡直快被烤焦了，這時你就可以回答他說 Tell me about it!，這句話意思就是，我知道你在說什麼，我也剛經歷過你說的情形。

46

think
[θɪŋk]

一個人對某件事情有特定的看法或想法就是 think，所以問對方的意見，就要問對方 **What do you think?**。公司裡有人想請約翰來做業務工作，你認為約翰不適合，你就該說 **I don't** think 約翰適合這個工作，你這也是在表達你對這件事情的看法。

動詞三態 think, thought, thought

精選例句

認為

認為

* I don't think it's right.

（我不認為那是對的。）

* I don't think John is fit for the job.

（我不認為約翰適合這個工作。）

* Do you think this car can last on such a long trip?

（你認為這部車子可以跑這麼一趟旅程嗎？）

* I think I'll go to Europe this summer.
（我想我今年夏天會去歐洲。）

* Do you think I should buy this book?
（你認為我應該買這本書嗎？）

* Who do you think will win?
（你認為誰會贏？）

想到

* I had never thought of becoming an actor.
我從未想過要當演員。）

用腦子去想

* He was trying to think what to do.
他在想該怎麼做。）

* I can't tell you now. I'll have to think about it.
我現在不能告訴你，我得想一想。）

你如果找不到鑰匙，又想不起來，到底放那兒去了，要說「我想不起來」的英語就是 **I can't think** 後面加上你想不起來的那件事。

◆ I can't think where I left my keys.
（我想不起來我把鑰匙放在哪裡。）

I think so.
（我認為可以。）

● 老闆交給你們這一組人一個企畫案，要你們這個週末前做完，接到了這個企畫案，有人就問了，週末前我們趕得出來嗎？如果你認為可以，你的回答就是 I think so.，如果你認為做不到，就可以回答 I don't think so.（我認為不能。）

What do you think?
（你認為怎麼樣？）

● 有人提出一個企畫案給你的老闆看，老闆看完了，先表示意見說，Well, I like it.（我喜歡這個企畫案。），然後，轉頭問你的意見 What do you think?（你認為怎麼樣？）

● 瑪麗買了一件漂亮的洋裝，興沖沖的跑來問你 What do you think?，你最好告訴她，這件洋裝很漂亮，你喜歡，人家錢已經花了，讓她高興高興吧。

這句話英語怎麼說

👉 要去上班，車子卻發不動，你說，車子發不動，這句話英語怎麼說？

👉 早上來上班，卻不見約翰，你知道他昨晚熬夜到很晚，這句話英語怎麼說？

👉 你想到瑪麗家過夜，你問媽媽，可以到瑪麗家過夜嗎，這句話英語怎麼說？

👉 你到店裡去買東西，你想用信用卡付錢，你要問他們有沒有收信用卡，這句話英語怎麼說？

👉 你跟朋友要分手，你跟他說再見之後，又叮嚀一句要他保重，這句話英語怎麼說？

這句話英語怎麼說

* 車子不發動。　　　　　　The car won't start.

* 約翰昨晚熬到很晚。　　　John stayed up late last night.

* 我可以到瑪麗家過夜嗎？　Can I stay over at Mary's?

* 你們收信用卡嗎？　　　　Do you take credit cards?

* 保重。　　　　　　　　　Take care.

47

try
[traɪ]

你不知道你做不做的到，但是你可以 try 看看，人家邀請你去參加他的宴會，你不知道有沒有空去，但是你答應 try 看看；你的脾氣太壞了，朋友勸你 try to 控制你的脾氣；你天天遲到，老師很生氣罵你，但是你也沒把握不遲到，只好跟老師說你會 try 不要遲到。科學家發明了新藥，在讓人類使用之前，要先在老鼠身上 try 看看，有效才可以用在人類的身上。你去餐廳吃飯，吃到一道菜很好吃，趕緊跟你的朋友說，這道菜很好吃，你一定要 try。至於約翰被抓去審判，要根據法律商議他有沒有罪，約翰就是 was tried（被審判）。

動詞三態 try, tried, tried

精選例句

試著做某件事

* I don't know if I can come but I'll try.
（我不知道我能不能來，但是我會盡量。）

* You must try to control your temper.
（你必須試著控制你的脾氣。）

* He tried moving the bookshelf alone, but it was too heavy.
（他試著自己移動書架，但是書架太重了。）

* I'll try not to be late again.
（我會試著不要再遲到。）

* She may not be good at singing, but at least she tries.
（她可能不會唱歌，但是至少她試了。）

做試驗、嘗試

* Scientists are trying the new drugs on rats.
（科學家在老鼠身上試驗新的藥。）

* Mary likes to try anything new.
（瑪莉喜歡嘗試新的東西。）

試吃某樣東西

* Would you like to try some raw fish?
（你要不要吃生魚片看看？）

* Have you tried this dish?
  （你有沒有嚐過這道菜？）

* You must try that dish.
  （那一道菜你一定要嚐嚐看。）

* Here, try this lemonade.
  （喏，這杯檸檬汁你看味道怎麼樣。）

試試看

* Could you try again later?
  （你稍後再試試看好嗎？）

* Try the other door. It may not be locked.
  （試試另一扇門，它或許沒上鎖。）

審訊

* John was tried for murder and found guilty.
  （約翰以謀殺罪被審判，而且被判有罪。）

try on	試穿

■ Did you try it on before you bought it?
（你買之前有沒有試穿？）

↻ 台灣留學生剛來美國，通常都很克難，要添購家具，大半不會一下子就全部買新的，老留學生多半會建議你 try garage sale 看看，你要買舊東西，人家建議你 try 某個地方的意思就是，要你到那個地方去看看，有沒有你正想買的東西。

- If you want to buy an old lamp, try garage sales.
  （如果你想買個舊燈，到「車庫拍賣」試試看。）

↻ 約翰的車子壞了，送到修車行去修理，要上班需要有人載他去，你知道同事瑪麗家在約翰家附近，你就建議約翰 try Mary，意思就是建議約翰問問瑪麗看看能不能載他去公司。

- Why don't you try Mary?
  Maybe she can give you a ride.
  （你何不問瑪麗看看？或許她能載你。）

48

turn
[tɝn]

當你轉動任何東西的時候，你就是在 turn 那樣東西；你如果推動車子，輪子就會開始 turn。人轉動身體，或是轉頭，都是在 turn；老師上課時會叫你把書翻到第幾頁，翻書的翻，英語也是 turn。小溪流啊流，有時流到某個地方就會開始 turn 往別的方向繼續流。

動詞三態 turn, turned, turned

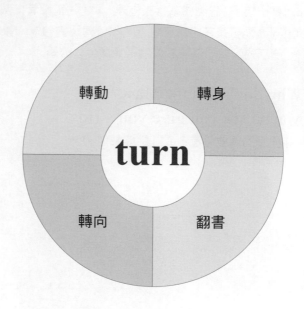

轉動

* She turned the key in the lock.
（她轉動鎖上面的鑰匙。）

* He pushed the cart and the wheels began to turn.
（他推動推車，輪子就開始轉動。）

轉身

* She turned her head away.
（她把頭轉開。）

* He turned and ran away.
（他轉身跑開。）

* Turn around and face me.
（轉過來，面對著我。）

* She turned to look back at him as she got on the train.
（當她上火車的時候，轉過來看他。）

* Turn to the left.
turn（轉到左邊。）

翻書

* Turn to page 10.
（翻到第十頁。）

轉向

* The river turns north at this point.
（這條河在這個地方轉向北流。）

turn （轉變）	sour（變酸）
	color（變顏色）
	pink（變粉紅色）
	red（變紅）
	gray（變灰色）

■ The milk turned sour.
（牛奶變酸。）

■ The leaves turn color in the fall.
（樹葉在秋天變顏色。）

■ The clothes all turned pink in the wash.
（衣服在洗的時候，通通變成粉紅色。）

■ She turned red when John teased her.
（約翰取笑她的時候，她臉上變紅。）

■ Her hair is starting to turn gray.
（她的頭髮開始變成灰色。）

turn 輕鬆學

☐ It's late. I think I'll turn in.
很晚了。我要去睡覺了。

☐ Did you turn in your paper yet?
你的報告交了沒有？

☐ Please turn off the lights when you leave.
你要離開的時候，請把燈關掉。

☐ What time are the street lights turned on?
街燈幾點開？

☐ I hope everything turns out all right.
我希望結果還令人滿意。

每天五分鐘

⏱ turn in 就是「上床睡覺」的意思。

⏱ turn in 也可以做「把東西交給某人」的意思。

⏱ turn off 是個片語，意思是「關燈、關電器」。

⏱ turn on 是 turn off 的相反詞，意思是「開燈、開電器」，例如：turn on TV（開電視），turn on the radio（開收音機）。

⏱ turn out 就是「結果是」的意思。

49

use
[juz]

我們 use 我們的手拿東西，use 我們的嘴巴吃飯。use 就是「使用某樣東西」的意思，我們也 use 我們的聰明來解決問題；use（使用）材料來使我們的東西改進，use 工具來幫助我們做事。我們用某間房子用來做儲藏室，就是我們 use 這個房子來做儲藏室不僅僅我們使用工具，使用材料是 use，利用別人也是在 use 別人。

動詞三態 use, used, used

精選例句

使用

* Have you ever used this software before?
  （你以前有沒有用過這個軟體？）

* We used a carrot for the snowman's nose.
  （我們用紅蘿蔔做雪人的鼻子。）

* We use this room for storing old books.

（我們用這個房間來儲藏舊書。）

* He used his intelligence to solve problems.

（他用他的聰明去解決問題。）

* What do you use to make your lawn so green?

（你用什麼東西，使你的草地這麼青翠？）

利用別人　* He uses others to do his dirty work for him.

（他利用別人替他做非法的事。）

use up	把某樣東西全部用玩

■ Who used up the last of the toothpaste?
（誰把牙膏通通用完？）

get used to	適應

■ Have you gotten used to the weather yet?
（你適應這種天氣了嗎？）

I could use a hand.

● 如果你要搬家，朋友問你需要什麼嗎，你覺得你需要幫忙，你可以回答說 I could use a hand.，句子中的 could use 某樣東西的意思就是，如果有這樣東西，那可真好，我正用得上。I could use a hand. 就是「如果你能幫忙，那可真好，我正需要」的意思。

● 大熱天，你在外面奔波了一天，熱得滿頭大汗，一回到家，老婆體貼的問你，回來啦，需要什麼東西嗎，你可以回答她說，I could use a soda.（我正需要一瓶汽水。）

Can I use your phone?

● 這句話是用在「要向別人借東西使用時」，例如：你要借電話，就該說 Can I use your phone?，如果你想跟對方借電腦一用，就跟他說 Can I use your computer?（我可以用你的電腦嗎？）

 這句話英語怎麼說

- 在時裝店，你看到一件很漂亮的洋裝，在買之前，你打算先試穿，你要跟店員說，我想試穿這件洋裝，這句話英語怎麼說？

- 在宴會上，你吃到一道菜很好吃，趕緊跟其他的人說，這道菜很好吃，你一定要嚐嚐，這句話英語怎麼說？

- 老師要開始上課，他跟同學說，翻到第十頁，這句話英語怎麼說？

- 夜已深，你打算去睡覺了，你要跟其他的人說，我想我要去睡覺了，這句話英語怎麼說？

- 你妹妹要去洗澡，等她洗完你也要去洗，你怕她把熱水全用光了，所以趕快叮嚀她一聲，別把熱水全用光了，這句話英語怎麼說？

這句話英語怎麼說

✳ 我想試穿這件洋裝。	I'd like to try on the dress.
✳ 這一道菜你一定得嚐嚐。	You must try the dish.
✳ 翻到第十頁。	Turn to page 10.
✳ 我想我該去睡覺了。	I think I'll turn in.
✳ 別把熱水用光。	Don't use up all the hot water.

50

watch
[watʃ]

當一個人在 watch 的時候，他不僅僅「看東西」而已，他是在注意看，而且不是隨便看一下就走，而是待在那兒一段時間在看，有「觀看」的意思，所以，看電視、看足球賽、甚至於看著小朋友在遊樂場所玩，都是在 watch。因為 watch 有「用心、注意看」的意思，所以，叫人家小心，英語的說法是 watch out；請人家照看一下孩子，也就是請他 watch the kids。

動詞三態 watch,watched,watched

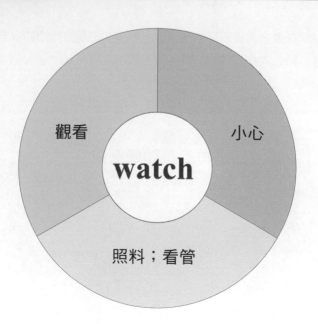

觀看 小心

watch

照料；看管

精選例句

觀看

* Do you want to watch TV at home or go to the movies?

（你要在家裡看電視，還是去看電影？）

* They are watching the football game.

（他們在看足球賽。）

* She watched the children play in the playground.

（她看著小朋友在遊樂場遊玩。）

* Watch carefully while I show you how to run the computer.

（我教你如何用電腦的時候，你要用心看。）

小心

* Watch that you don't drop the camera.

（小心照相機不要摔了。）

**照料；
看管**

* Can you watch the kids while I am away?

（我不在的時候你可以看著孩子們嗎？）

* Could you watch my books for me while I go to the restroom?

（我去洗手間的時候，可不可以請你幫我看一下我的書本？）

有一個小朋友要穿過馬路，你一眼瞥見有輛車子疾駛而來，這時你應該大聲的對著那個小朋友叫道 watch out，意思是叫對方「小心」。

◆ Watch out! There's a car coming!
（小心！有部車子來了！）

看電視的英語是 watch TV，看報紙的英語是 read the newspaper，而去看電影則是說 go to the movies。

◆ Mary and John are watching TV.
（瑪麗和約翰在看電視。）

◆ Daddy reads the newspaper after breakfast.
（父親早餐後就看報紙。）

◆ We went to the movies last night.
（我們昨晚去看電影。）

51

work
[wɜk]

在上班或是工作都是在 work，加班就是 work overtime；機器或是物件沒有壞，就是那個機器 works（可以用），相反的，若是壞了不能用，就是那機器或物件 doesn't work；一個計畫或是主意行得通，就表示那個計畫或是主意 works。約翰要在他的車子上裝一個新的音響系統，現在正在外面 working on hiscar。

動詞三態 work, worked, worked

精選例句

上班

* John is 80, and still working.
  （約翰已經八十歲，還在上班。）

* I work overtime a lot.
  （我常加班。）

* There's no way I'm working Sundays.
  （我絕不在星期天上班。）

* I've been working long hours lately.
  （最近我工作時間很長。）

* Mary isn't working tomorrow.
  （瑪莉明天不上班。）

* My sister works in a law firm.
（我妹妹在一家律師事務所上班。）

* Mary works in that office building.
（瑪莉在那棟辦公大樓裡上班。）

work	在某個公司上班	做事情
	機器運轉正常	有效；行得通

**在某個
公司上班**

* She's been working for IBM for years now.
（她已經在 IBM 上班多年。）

* John works for Microsoft I believe.
（約翰應該是在微軟公司上班。）

* Mary works for either Nations Banks or Bank of America.
（瑪莉不是在國家銀行就是在美國銀行上班。）

* John works as a chemical engineer at Dupont.
（約翰在杜邦公司擔任石化工程師。）

做事情

* He is working on his car outside.
（他在外面忙著他的車子。）

* She's been working all day in the kitchen.
（已經在廚房裡忙了一整天。）

機器運轉 正常

* The telephone is not working.
（電話壞了。）

* My microwave has not been working since I bought it.
（我的微波爐自從我買回來以後，一直是壞的。）

有效、 行得通

* Will the plan work?
（這個計畫行得通嗎？）

* I don't think his idea will work.
（我不認為他的主意行得通。）

國家圖書館出版品預行編目資料

5 分鐘征服英文法 / 張瑪麗著 . -- 新北市：哈
福企業有限公司, 2022.05
面；　公分 . --（英語系列；79）
ISBN 978-626-95576-8-4(平裝附光碟片)
1.CST: 英語　2.CST: 語法
805.16　　　　　　　　111006247

英語系列：79

. . . .

書名 / 5 分鐘征服英文法
作者 / 張瑪麗
出版單位 / 哈福企業有限公司
責任編輯 /Joyce Chou
封面設計 / 李秀英
內文排版 / 八十文創
出版者／哈福企業有限公司
地址／新北市板橋區五權街 16 號 1 樓
電話／ (02) 2808-4587 傳真／ (02) 2808-6545
郵政劃撥／ 31598840 戶名／哈福企業有限公司
出版日期／ 2022 年 5 月
定價／ NT$ 340 元 (附 MP3)
港幣定價／ 113 元 (附 MP3)
封面內文圖 / 取材自 Shutterstock

. . . .

全球華文國際市場總代理／采舍國際有限公司
地址／新北市中和區中山路 2 段 366 巷 10 號 3 樓
電話／ (02) 8245-8786 傳真／ (02) 8245-8718
網址／ www.silkbook.com 新絲路華文網

. . . .

香港澳門總經銷／和平圖書有限公司
地址／香港柴灣嘉業街 12 號百樂門大廈 17 樓
電話／ (852) 2804-6687 傳真／ (852) 2804-6409

. . . .

email ／ welike8686@Gmail.com
網址／ Haa-net.com
facebook ／ Haa-net 哈福網路商城

. . . .

Original Copyright © AA Bridgers Co., Ltd.
著作權所有　翻印必究
如有破損或裝訂缺頁，請寄回本公司更換

電子書格式：PDF

哈福

哈福